"I don't know the first thing about being a parent."

Neither did Audrey. However, some things were instinctive. "As long as you give her what she needs most of all, the rest will come."

He glanced across the center console. "And what is that?"

"Love."

The lines in his brow relaxed. "Thanks. You always were good at putting things in perspective for me."

Her heart thudded against her ribs. Was that why he'd simply gone on as though nothing had changed after her miscarriage? Allowed a chasm to grow between them that had been too big for her tattered heart to breach? Because she hadn't *told* him she was grieving the loss of their child.

She stared straight ahead. *He'll be gone soon enough.* All she had to do was sign that listing agreement, and he'd be on his way.

Publishers Weekly bestselling author **Mindy Obenhaus** lives on a ranch in Texas with her husband, two sassy pups, and countless cattle and deer. She's passionate about touching readers with biblical truths in an entertaining, and sometimes adventurous, manner. When she's not writing, you'll usually find her in the kitchen, spending time with family or roaming the ranch. She'd love to connect with you via her website, mindyobenhaus.com.

Books by Mindy Obenhaus

Love Inspired

Legacy Ranch

An Unexpected Companion
Their Texas Christmas Redemption

Hope Crossing

The Cowgirl's Redemption
A Christmas Bargain
Loving the Rancher's Children
Her Christmas Healing
Hidden Secrets Between Them
Rediscovering Christmas

Bliss, Texas

A Father's Promise
A Brother's Promise
A Future to Fight For
Their Yuletide Healing

Visit the Author Profile page at LoveInspired.com for more titles.

THEIR TEXAS CHRISTMAS REDEMPTION

MINDY OBENHAUS

LOVE INSPIRED
INSPIRATIONAL ROMANCE

If you purchased this book without a cover you should be aware that this book is stolen property. It was reported as "unsold and destroyed" to the publisher, and neither the author nor the publisher has received any payment for this "stripped book."

LOVE INSPIRED®
INSPIRATIONAL ROMANCE

ISBN-13: 978-1-335-23017-1

Their Texas Christmas Redemption

Copyright © 2025 by Melinda Obenhaus

All rights reserved. No part of this book may be used or reproduced in any manner whatsoever without written permission.

Without limiting the author's and publisher's exclusive rights, any unauthorized use of this publication to train generative artificial intelligence (AI) technologies is expressly prohibited.

This is a work of fiction. Names, characters, places and incidents are either the product of the author's imagination or are used fictitiously. Any resemblance to actual persons, living or dead, businesses, companies, events or locales is entirely coincidental.

For questions and comments about the quality of this book, please contact us at CustomerService@Harlequin.com.

® is a trademark of Harlequin Enterprises ULC.

Love Inspired
22 Adelaide St. West, 41st Floor
Toronto, Ontario M5H 4E3, Canada
www.LoveInspired.com

Printed in U.S.A.

The Lord is nigh unto them that are of a broken heart; and saveth such as be of a contrite spirit.
—*Psalms* 34:18

For Your Glory, Lord

Chapter One

Moving to Legacy Ranch was supposed to mark a new beginning. Instead, Audrey Caldwell was about to come face-to-face with her past.

She paced the long-leaf pine floorboards between the two-story colonial farmhouse's living and dining room Tuesday afternoon, a tempest of emotions pulsing through her every fiber. Tyler was due here any moment. Per their divorce decree, her ex-husband had continued to live in the house they'd purchased only weeks after marrying seven years ago. Now—four years after their divorce—he was ready to sell the historic bungalow they'd painstakingly renovated and needed her signature on the listing agreement in order to do so. Something that could've easily been done by mail, yet he'd driven all the way from Fort Worth to Houston, only to discover she no longer worked at the commercial real estate firm her father had presided over until his death earlier this year.

Now Tyler was on his way to Legacy Ranch.

Situated a little more than an hour northwest of Houston, the land that boasted three thousand acres of rolling hills and picturesque watering holes had been in her family for more than a hundred and fifty years. The bucolic setting had always been a haven for Audrey, but as of last Saturday, she now called it home. One she shared with her father's sister, D'Lynn Hunt, aka Aunt Dee, who ran the cattle ranch, as well as Audrey's second-eldest sister, Tessa, along with Tessa's nine-year-old son, Grayson, and six-year-old Bryce, who'd moved here this past summer. And if things played out the way she hoped, Audrey might soon be adding her own child to the mix.

Since their father's death, Audrey had been taking stock of her life. A life that seemed to revolve around her work as a commercial real estate agent. Yet while she'd been successful in her endeavors, her life felt empty. Unfulfilled. So, after watching Tessa take a leap of faith, Audrey decided to shake things up, too.

She'd announced her intentions to her three sisters the day after Tessa's engagement party last month. And effective yesterday, she stepped into her new position as director of ranch growth, overseeing various projects as a portion of the land was transformed into a relaxing getaway and retreat destination. One that would eventually include tent cabins—part tent, part cabin— for the ultimate glamping experience, as well as a venue for weddings and other events. Given Legacy Ranch's proximity to both Houston and Austin, she had no doubt it would be a success.

The best thing of all was that her new lifestyle would be more conducive to motherhood. After years of wishing and wondering, she was ready to set the wheels in motion to adopt and fulfill her dream of becoming a mother. A dream that had been squashed after a heartbreaking miscarriage and her subsequent divorce. And while she'd shared her intentions to adopt with Aunt Dee, she had yet to reveal the painful truth behind her divorce.

Now Tyler's impending arrival brought back memories of failure and loss. Memories she'd tried to forget. But losing a baby you desperately wanted wasn't something that was easily forgotten.

Movement outside the living room window had her pausing atop the cream and blue area rug. Then she glimpsed a graphite-colored crew cab pickup truck easing toward the front of the house.

Turning, she darted from the living room to the adjoining dining room and into the quintessential farmhouse kitchen with mismatched cabinets and worn lemon-yellow countertops. The last thing she wanted was Tyler thinking she was eager to see him. On the contrary, all she wanted was to sign that document and send him on his way. Not that she wasn't a little bit curious as to why he was selling the once-rundown house they'd fallen in love with the first time they laid eyes on it. Had he found someone else? Remarried?

Her heart pinched. Maybe he had a family. A growing one that needed more space.

She looked up at the wood-plank ceiling and pulled in a deep breath. So what if Tyler had moved on? She had, too. And she was super excited to see what this new phase of her life might hold.

She glanced at her watch. What was taking him so long? Maybe he was on the phone. She wasn't about to look, though. She just needed to be patient—

A knock at the front door had her lifting her chin a notch. She strolled from the kitchen into the center hall and past the stairs until she reached the solid-wood door at the other end. Then, with a deep breath and a smile she didn't feel, she twisted the knob and swung the door open.

Seeing the only man she'd ever loved standing on the other side, wearing medium-wash jeans that fit just right and a russet T-shirt that emphasized biceps larger than she recalled, had her holding tightly to the doorknob. No doubt about it, Tyler was as handsome as ever—if not more so—with his thick dark brown hair mussed just so. Though the heavy-stubble beard was new, it looked as though it belonged. Yet sadness seemed to overshadow the usual glimmer in his light brown eyes. It was a look she hadn't seen before. Not even when she'd miscarried the child they'd longed for.

She lowered her gaze. That was when she noticed the infant carrier he held with one hand. Inside it, beneath a pale pink blanket, a tiny bundle slept. With wisps of fine brown hair, pink cheeks and seemingly pouting lips, the sight unleashed a longing Audrey would do well to get a grip on.

But where was the child's mother? Why wouldn't Tyler have left the baby with her? He'd never been a spiteful person. Yet he came to see her with an infant in tow?

When she looked at him again, he rubbed his forehead with a shaky hand. "It's good to see you, Audrey."

She wished she could say the same. But given the inner turmoil his presence had unleashed, she simply nodded and motioned him inside.

He whisked past her, and as she closed the door, she noticed a pale pink and gray backpack slung over his shoulder, as if he was planning to hang around for a while. Then again, when babies were involved, it was always good to be prepared. Or so she'd heard.

"We can go in the living room." She gestured to the room just off the center hall, preferring to keep things formal. Businesslike.

"Wow!" He took in the recently renovated space. "This looks nothing like I remember. It's so bright." He looked her way. "Didn't there used to be dark paneling in here?"

She nodded. "Until a few months ago. Tessa was prepared to paint over it until she learned there was shiplap hidden underneath. Uncovering it became her summer project."

"Is Nick still in the military?" Nick was Tessa's late husband.

Audrey shook her head. "He passed away a few years ago, after suffering a traumatic brain injury in Afghanistan." She didn't feel the need to mention Nick had taken his own life.

"I'm sorry to hear that. I always liked Nick."

She nodded. "Tessa and the boys live here now. She's getting married in March."

His brow shot up. "No kidding? That's great she was able to find happiness again."

After what Tessa had gone through, she deserved to be happy. She and her boys. "Yes, it is."

A whimper came from the infant seat, followed by a blood-curdling cry.

"I'm sorry." Tyler set the carrier on the floor and knelt beside it, the backpack slipping to the floor as he unhooked the unhappy baby. "I was hoping she'd stay asleep." Making a shushing sound, he fumbled with the harness. "It's okay, sweetheart."

The tenderness in his tone had Audrey recalling the countless scenarios she'd played out in her mind after learning she was pregnant. Envisioning Tyler tenderly cradling their child, teaching him or her to ride a bike.

Yet she hadn't seen anything even resembling grief from him when she miscarried. And his placating words, like "It wasn't meant to be," had felt like sandpaper on an open wound.

With the child now in his arms, clad in a pink onesie, he turned her so Audrey could see her face. "This is Willow."

If it were anyone else's baby, Audrey would've had no problem engaging. But this one had Tyler's eyes.

She looked away. "So, do you have that paperwork for me to sign?" She wasn't sure how much more her heart could take. Did Tyler even realize how this whole scenario was impacting her?

Probably not. Tyler was all about Tyler. His wants and needs. Not those of a grieving wife.

"I do." Bouncing the once-again fussy infant, he retrieved the backpack from the floor and set it atop the side chair. Then he fumbled to unzip it with one hand while Willow's crying continued to escalate. "If I can just—"

"Are you sure she's not hungry?" As if Audrey was some sort of expert.

"Maybe." He pulled a bottle from the backpack's side pocket. "She hasn't really eaten much today." After giving it a shake, he removed the lid.

"Don't you need to heat it up?" Why was she

offering advice? He was the child's father. He'd known better than her.

He sent her a fretful look. "Would you mind?"

Shaking her head, she turned for the kitchen. "Follow me." After retrieving a saucepan from the cupboard, she filled it halfway with water before putting it on the stove to heat.

As she added the bottle, Willow's cries grew louder, her face redder.

You could offer to help the poor guy.

"I'm sorry." Holding the wailing child to his shoulder, he bounced her.

Hoping to hurry things along, Audrey removed the bottle from the pan, shook it and tested the formula on her wrist. When it was still cold, she returned it to the stove. "Does she have a pacifier?"

Still bobbing, he started back into the living room. "Yeah, but I'm not sure where it is."

Foolishly, she followed. Then watched as he grabbed the backpack, awkwardly holding a now-screaming Willow while he fumbled with the bag.

Would you help the poor fella already? If not for him, then for the baby's sake.

Audrey hated it when her internal voice sounded like Aunt Dee.

She sucked in a breath and reached for the child. "Let me hold her while you search." No point in committing to anything lengthy.

"Are you sure?"

"Yes."

Meeting her gaze, he placed Willow in her arms. "Thank you."

Audrey cradled the tiny bundle in the crook of her arm and patted her little bottom as she returned to the kitchen to make sure the bottle didn't overheat. "There, there, now. You're alright. You have to be patient with us grown-ups sometimes because we haven't learned to speak your language."

To her surprise, Willow quieted. And stared up at her with eyes that were so like Tyler's.

"Let's check that bottle, shall we?" Retrieving it from the water, she gave it a gentle shake before testing it again. "I'm no expert, but I think this should be to your liking." Audrey offered the bottle to Willow, who greedily began sucking.

"Ah, music to my ears." Tyler joined them, looking more than a little frazzled.

All of a sudden, Willow spit out the bottle. Her face contorted and she began to cry once again, her hands flailing around her ears.

Setting the bottle on the counter, Audrey lifted the baby to her shoulder and began patting her back. "Maybe she's gassy from all that crying." Why did she keep repeating all these things she'd heard other women say, yet knew nothing about?

She shifted between patting and rubbing, hoping to coax something from the infant. "Come on, Willow. Let it out." She set her cheek atop Willow's head. And as heat radiated into her own skin, she looked at Tyler. "This baby's got a fever."

Tyler Caldwell knew nothing about babies. Zip. Zero. Zilch. Yet that hadn't stopped him from saying "of course" when his sister, Carrie, had asked him if he would agree to be Willow's guardian in the event anything happened to her. After all, he and Carrie were all that was left of their family, and they were young.

When he'd signed that document, he never could've imagined that only a few weeks later his sister would be gone, leaving him to raise her newborn daughter. A child he'd barely even held, despite little Willow and her mama living under his roof. Willow was so tiny, and he was afraid he might do something wrong.

Now, while he still struggled with how to change a diaper and how much and what to feed his niece, Willow was sick. And he wasn't even aware.

No wonder she'd slept the majority of what had turned into a seven-hour road trip. Not to mention cried her way through her last feeding. And yet he'd taken it as a good sign when she'd fallen back to sleep once they'd started moving again.

He watched Audrey sway back and forth. "Fever? What do you think is wrong with her?"

She frowned. "How would I know? I'm not an expert on babies."

Did that mean she hadn't remarried? Or, if she had, she apparently didn't have any children. Not that it was any business of his. He'd failed Audrey as a husband. So just like his father, his mother, and now Carrie, Audrey had left him.

Making him even more determined to do right by Willow. Though he was off to a lousy start. Despite the stack of baby books on his nightstand, he had yet to get through a single one. Every time he started reading, he'd fall asleep. Only to be awakened by a hungry Willow a few hours later.

Now, as her cries morphed into a pathetic moan, her eyes grew heavy. And soon the distinctive tick-tock of the old schoolhouse clock across the room was the only sound that could be heard.

Audrey heaved a sigh. "How come you didn't leave Willow with her mother?" She obviously thought Willow was his daughter. Then again, Carrie had said Willow had his eyes.

He swallowed the sudden lump in his throat. "Because she's dead."

Audrey's chestnut brown eyes widened.

"She's my sister's daughter. Carrie was killed in a car accident three weeks ago." He dragged his fingers through his hair. "Thankfully, she'd taken legal measures to ensure Willow would be cared for. Sadly, the poor kid is stuck with me. Bumbling imbecile that I am." Stepping closer, he brushed his pinky finger over Willow's tiny fist. A second later, her hand opened just enough to take hold of his finger.

Audrey's expression softened as she peered up at him. She still smelled like sunshine and wildflowers. "What about Willow's father?"

Tyler shook his head, taking in the comforting kitchen where he'd once shared many a meal. "Carrie never mentioned anyone, and I didn't press her. He's listed as 'unknown' on the birth certificate." Something that didn't necessarily surprise him. With their father out of the picture and their mother barely around, a twenty-year-old Tyler had been left to care for his then-seventeen-year-old sister after their mother died. Carrie had taken off at the first opportunity—and ended up getting involved in drugs.

One of the happiest days of Tyler's life was when she showed up at his house several months ago, drug-free, pregnant and filled with a newfound faith.

Gently patting Willow, Audrey continued to watch him. "You know, you could've just mailed me the form."

Suddenly uncomfortable, he shoved his hands in the pockets of his jeans and moved to stand on the other side of the vintage butcher block island.

"I know. But I wanted to explain everything and make sure you didn't have any objections."

"Explain what? I'm a real estate agent. Besides, ever hear of a telephone?"

"I was afraid you might not answer." They hadn't talked since that day in court when their divorce was finalized. Come to think of it, they hadn't spoken then, either. Only through their attorneys.

Her brow puckered as she continued to watch him. "So you didn't even bother trying? Yet you set out on a road trip with a newborn?"

Yes, he had. Because for whatever reason—maybe it had to do with Carrie's death or needing closure—he'd wanted to see Audrey one last time.

"Between grief and lack of sleep, my mind's been pretty messed up lately." He heaved a sigh. "That's why I took a leave of absence from my company."

Her gaze narrowed as she continued to sway back and forth with Willow. "Are you still doing real estate?"

"No, construction." The less intimidating topic had him looking her way. "My partner suggested I take a few months off to sort out my—*our*—lives." Two decades older than Tyler's thirty-four years, Reid Morrison was more than a business partner, he was Tyler's best friend and mentor.

A Godly man who'd breathed spiritual truth into Tyler's sorry existence after Audrey left.

"That's why I'm selling the house. I need more space and a yard for Willow to run around in. Well, whenever she can walk, that is. And good schools." He sighed. "Honestly, it's overwhelming."

For a moment, he thought he glimpsed a shimmer of compassion in Audrey's eyes. Not that he deserved it. He hadn't shown her any when she'd miscarried. Instead, he'd refused to let himself feel anything. The same way he had when his father abandoned him, his mother and his sister when Tyler was seven. And again when his mother died. Now, with Carrie gone, he'd been so busy trying to determine how to move forward, he hadn't had time to think about anything but caring for Willow.

And now he was failing at that, too.

Sounds from the laundry room had him and Audrey looking that way as Audrey's aunt Dee entered, along with Nash, her tricolored blue merle Australian shepherd.

"Whose truck's that out front?" While the dog continued toward Tyler and Audrey, the sixty-something, forever-blond rancher removed her straw cowboy hat and toed out of her boots before continuing into the kitchen clad in faded jeans and a chambray shirt over a pink tee. "I didn't recognize—" Her faded blue eyes widened when she saw Tyler petting Nash. "Well, I'll be." A slow grin had the corners of her mouth lifting as she approached. "Tyler Caldwell."

Straightening, he extended his hand. "Good to see you, Ms. D'Lynn."

With her shoulder-length hair pulled back into a low ponytail, she glanced from his hand to his face, her gaze narrowing. "That's Aunt Dee to you, young man. And you know I prefer a hug over a handshake any day."

Holding out his arms, he felt his cheeks heating. "I didn't want to assume anything." His six-foot frame all but dwarfed the petite woman as she wrapped her arms around his torso. It was the best thing he'd felt in a long while.

"What are you doin'—?"

Willow's mournful cry had the woman jerking her attention to Audrey.

"Oh, my." Moving beside her niece, Aunt Dee palmed the baby's head. "Why, you're just a tee-niney little thing. How'd you get here?"

"This is Tyler's niece, Willow," said Audrey. "And I think she has a fever."

Aunt Dee tenderly pressed her lips to the infant's head. "She sure does." Her expression suddenly serious, she looked from Audrey to Tyler and back. "Has she been to the doctor?"

"No, ma'am." Tyler inched closer. "I wasn't even aware something was wrong until Audrey mentioned the fever a few minutes ago."

"Where's her mama?" The older woman looked genuinely concerned. But then, that was Aunt Dee for you.

"She passed away. I'm Willow's guardian."

Without flinching, Aunt Dee turned back to the baby. "In that case, I suggest the two of you load this little one into your truck and get her to the urgent care in Hope Crossing before they close."

"Both of us?" Audrey's voice took on a higher pitch.

"Of course." Her aunt nodded. "You'll need to show him where it is."

"I know where Hope Crossing is, but not the urgent care." Audrey looked almost indignant.

"Oh, as if anyone could get lost in Hope Crossing. It's right there on the corner at the blinking light." Aunt Dee pulled her phone from her back pocket. "Now, get that little one ready to go while I call and let 'em know you're on your way."

With Aunt Dee on their heels, Tyler followed Audrey into the dining room, well aware that she did not want to accompany him any more than she wanted gangrene.

In the living room, Audrey stooped to settle Willow into her car seat, a curious Nash coming alongside her to sniff the baby.

"Y'all need to hurry now." Aunt Dee was more than a little insistent. "I'll let you know if there's a problem." Turning, Aunt Dee tapped her phone, then pressed it to her ear on her way back to the kitchen.

Audrey connected all the buckles so Willow was secure. Standing, she lifted her chin. "We'd better go before she chases us out with a broom."

"It's alright, Audrey. You don't need to come. I know how to get to Hope Crossing. And there's only one blinking light."

She glanced from him to Willow. "But what if she gets fussy on the ride?" Her eyes met his again. "That'll only worry you more. And I think you've had enough stress for one day."

Her compassion surprised him. "Are you sure?"

Audrey nodded. "Now, let's go before Aunt Dee gets off the phone and scolds us again."

Chapter Two

When Audrey had needed Tyler the most, he'd been emotionally unavailable. So sympathy was the last thing she wanted to feel for him. Little Willow, on the other hand…

Learning the baby had lost her mother touched something deep within Audrey. Though she'd been twelve and old enough to understand that her mother was never coming back when she'd died suddenly of an aneurism, the hole it had left in Audrey's heart was one few people, if anyone, could fill. Thankfully, she and her sisters had Aunt Dee to lovingly navigate them not only through their loss, but through all of life's bumps and bruises.

But who would be there for Willow?

Now the poor baby was sick. After receiving an ear infection diagnosis from the nurse practitioner at the urgent care, they drove to the pharmacy in Brenham to pick up the antibiotic and some fever reducer before returning to the ranch.

Thankfully, as long as the vehicle was moving, the baby slept.

"I can't believe she's sick, and I didn't even know it." While Willow continued to snooze in the back seat, Tyler had a death grip on the steering wheel as they approached the entrance to Legacy Ranch.

Eyeing Aunt Dee's longhorns grazing in the lush pasture on the opposite side of the split-rail fence, Audrey said, "I'm pretty sure you're not the first parent to say that."

"Parent?" He looked befuddled as he made the turn and maneuvered his Ford Super Duty over the cattle guard. "I'm not Willow's parent. That was Carrie's role."

Audrey faced him, willing an air of compassion into her voice. "Carrie's gone, Tyler. And she wanted *you* to raise her daughter. Willow is not going to grow up calling you her guardian."

He heaved a sigh, his shoulders drooping. "You're right. It's just…this is all so new and unexpected. I don't know the first thing about being a parent."

Neither did Audrey. However, some things were instinctive. "As long as you give her what she needs most of all, the rest will come."

He glanced across the center console. "And what is that?"

"Love."

The lines in his brow relaxed. "Thanks. You

always were good at putting things in perspective for me."

Her heart thudded against her ribs. Was that why he'd simply gone on as though nothing had changed after her miscarriage? Allowed a chasm to grow between them that had been too big for her tattered heart to breach? Because she hadn't *told* him she was grieving the loss of their child.

She stared straight ahead. *He'll be gone soon enough.* All she had to do was sign that listing agreement and he'd be on his way.

"In all the chaos, I haven't had time to ask what you're doing here at the ranch." He glanced from the winding dirt road to her. "The receptionist at your dad's office said you no longer worked there."

"That's correct. I moved here to help bring Aunt Dee's vision to life."

"You're going to be a rancher?" His expression held both confusion and disbelief.

"Ha! If you believe that, then you never knew me."

"You obviously missed my attempt at sarcasm."

She stared at her clasped hands resting atop her denim-covered lap as they bumped over another cattle guard. "My dad passed away earlier this year." Leaving her and her sisters a decent inheritance, as well as his half of Legacy Ranch. "The office hasn't been the same since."

Reaching across the center console, Tyler placed his larger hand over hers, his palm warm and calloused. "I'm sorry, Audrey. I had no idea."

For a moment, she just looked at him, the compassion in both his tone and those light brown eyes unexpected. "That's alright." She shrugged it off. "I didn't expect you would. But thank you."

When he removed his hand, she continued. "With Dad gone, my sisters and I now own half of the ranch while Aunt Dee has the rest. And apparently, she has some dreams for the place that she's kept to herself because our father would've just as soon sold off the land."

"What kind of dreams?"

"They're still evolving, but let's just say she wants to share a little bit of the ranch with others in hopes of making them smile."

"O-kay..." He kept his eyes on the dirt drive. "What does that look like?"

"Well, do you remember the log cabin?"

"You mean the hunting cabin?" They used to peek inside it occasionally when they'd go for walks. Back then, the rather crude structure had been just one room and a loft.

"That's the one. Aunt Dee had it transformed into a cozy getaway." One that now had both a kitchen and bathroom. "It's super cute. And the few guests it's hosted so far have left rave reviews." Reviews Audrey planned to use in their marketing.

"No kidding?" Tyler sounded more than a little enthused. "I'd love to see it."

Not likely, since that would only extend his visit.

As they neared the ranch house, Audrey spotted her sister Tessa's SUV in the drive, alongside her fiancé Dirk's truck.

Audrey glanced at her watch, surprised it was after five thirty. There was no way Tyler could travel back to Fort Worth with Willow tonight. Perhaps she should've suggested they look for a hotel when they were in Brenham.

Or they could stay at the ranch.

Nope. Not happening. That wasn't her call anyway.

Aunt Dee must've been watching for them, because Tyler had barely brought the truck to a stop when the front door opened, and she hurried down the steps with Nash on her heels.

Audrey pushed her door wide and hopped out, the late afternoon heat enveloping her as her aunt drew closer. Despite the calendar's claim it was autumn, it had yet to reach southeast Texas.

"Well—" Aunt Dee eyed Audrey while Tyler retrieved Willow from the back seat "—how'd it go?"

"She has an ear infection," said Audrey.

"Poor thing." Dee pouted. "I remember your mama sayin' how miserable you girls were whenever you'd get one of those."

Though Audrey's aunt never had children, she'd always had a close relationship with her nieces, even sacrificing her life here at the ranch to come and live with them in Houston after their mother died. Whether it was getting a bunch of scrappy ranch hands to do her bidding or raising four little girls ranging from age eight to sixteen, Aunt Dee had a way of making everything look easy.

"I need to give her some fever reducer and that antibiotic." Tyler approached, holding the car seat, and Audrey could hear Willow starting to whimper. "I have a feeling she's about to wind up again."

Aunt Dee peered down at the baby. "Of course she is. You're not feelin' good, are you darlin'?" She looked up at Tyler. "Mind if I take her out of this contraption?"

Lowering it to the ground, he said, "Be my guest. She may be setting up for another round of fussing, though."

"Dat's alright." Dee cooed as she unbuckled the baby, whose face was growing red. "I'm not afraid of a little cryin'." Lifting the child into her arms, she stood. "Supper's almost ready, so y'all come on in."

"Thank you, but I wasn't planning to stay." Tyler shifted from one booted foot to the other. "I'll just give Willow her medicine and feed her before we head back to Fort Worth."

Aunt Dee scowled. "You can't travel with a sick baby. I mean, how would you feel if you were sick, and someone took you on a long road trip?" She peered down at Willow. "She's had enough jostlin' for one day, haven't you, darlin'? You just need someplace to settle in for the night so you can rest."

Willow looked as though she was hanging on Aunt Dee's every word. Either that, or she was wondering who the goofy cowgirl was.

Audrey couldn't argue, though. Tyler looked spent. It would be better for both of them to get a good night's rest and start out fresh tomorrow.

"I suppose you're right." Tyler sighed. "I assume the closest hotel is in Brenham?"

"Yes, as far as I know." Audrey nodded.

"I'll hear of no such thing." Aunt Dee's narrowed gaze darted between them. "Not when we've got a perfectly wonderful cabin right here. Comfy bed, bathroom, one of those fancy coffeemakers that uses those overpriced pod thingies. I've even got a crib for Miss Willow." Looking at Audrey, she said, "You remember that portable one I had for Grayson and Bryce?"

Audrey nodded.

"It's in the closet upstairs in the middle bedroom. You'll need to make sure there's bedding with it."

"Yes, ma'am." Audrey's gaze darted to Tyler before falling to the grass. While she concurred that Willow shouldn't be traveling, she wished her aunt didn't feel the need to be so hospitable. At least if Tyler went to a hotel, Audrey wouldn't have to see him again tomorrow.

Though she supposed it would be nice to know how Willow was doing. After all, it usually took time for antibiotics to start working. And the thought of Willow's woeful cries earlier still tugged at Audrey's heart.

"I'd hate to impose." Tyler dragged his fingers through his hair. "We've done our fair share of that already."

"Nonsense. You're stayin' here, and that's final." Dee turned and started toward the house. "Now, y'all bring that baby's medicine so we can set her on the road to recovery."

When the sun rose the next morning, Tyler was beyond exhausted. While the cabin had all the luxuries one could ask for—including a comfortable queen-size bed—none of that mattered when there was a sick baby.

Willow's fever had been up and down all night. Whenever he tried to give her a bottle, she'd grab at her ears, inevitably scratching herself, which only made her cry more.

Finally, somewhere around 4:00 a.m., she'd dozed off. But when he attempted to put her in the crib Aunt Dee had prepared, she woke up and started crying all over again.

And here he thought he'd had everything figured out. It had seemed like such a good idea. He'd drive to Houston, get Audrey to sign the document, then turn around and head back to Fort Worth. He'd even gotten an early start. Then, as they approached Houston, everything started to fall apart.

Now, as he faced a new day, things weren't looking much better. Thankfully, he'd had enough forethought to toss a bunch of Willow's onesies and sleepers into the diaper bag, as well as pack a duffle for himself, just in case. Definitely a God thing.

In the cabin's small kitchen, he added another pod to the coffee machine while Willow finally slept in the crib. He'd need a lot of caffeine before they hit the road. He couldn't blame his lack of sleep solely on Willow, though. Thoughts of Audrey had commanded a fair amount of his attention, too. While he'd spent the last four years convincing himself their split had been for the best, it had taken less than an hour with her for him to realize what a coward he'd been, allowing her to walk out of his life.

Instead of grieving with her, he'd buried his feelings and hidden behind a mask of nonchalance just the way he'd taught his seven-year-old self to do when his father left. At the time, he'd told himself he had to be strong for Audrey. Since he'd started going to church, though, and more importantly, entered into a personal relationship with Jesus Christ, he'd come to realize that true strength was owning up to your weaknesses. Something he was obviously still learning.

A subtle rapping at the door pulled him from his thoughts. So quiet that if he hadn't been standing right there, he might not have heard it.

After eyeing his spit-up–stained T-shirt and basketball shorts, he took two steps in his bare feet, unlocked the door and eased it open.

Aunt Dee stood on the porch that was adorned with a couple of rocking chairs and large pots bearing fall-colored flowers in shades of russet, yellow and white, wearing her usual jeans, boots, work shirt and hat. Her hopeful expression evaporated the moment she looked at him. "Rough night?"

He dragged his fingers through his hair. "That obvious?"

Thrusting a large thermos toward him, she said, "I had a feelin' you might need this."

He took hold of it. "What is it?"

"Coffee. A whole lot more than that wimpy little contraption you've got in there can put out."

As the machine spit out the last of his brew, the corners of his mouth tugged with what he hoped was a smile, though he was too exhausted to know for certain. "I always knew you were a wise woman." He gestured to the container in his hand. "This proves my theory." Holding the door wider, he said, "Care to join me?"

"No, thanks." Her smile widened. "Though I wouldn't mind takin' a peek at that baby girl."

He stepped aside. "Be my guest." While Aunt Dee crossed to the portable crib behind the faux-leather sofa, he set the thermos on the counter and retrieved the freshly brewed cup from the "contraption," grinning at the sassy rancher's terminology.

Turning, he took a tentative sip while watching her stare at his niece. "I'm hoping to be out of your hair sometime early this afternoon."

Her brow pinched, she touched a hand to the child's head, her lips pursed. "I wouldn't advise that."

He inched closer, eyeing his niece, who seemed to be sleeping contentedly. "Why do you say that?"

Concerned blue eyes met his. "She's still got a fever."

He felt his body deflate. Not that he had much oomph in it to begin with. The last twenty-four hours had about sucked the life out of him. "But she's not due for more fever reducer for—" he glanced at his watch "—two hours."

The woman stepped toward him, shaking her head. "In the meantime, sleep is the best thing for her. It'll help her body heal."

"What if she wakes up?" He jabbed his fingers through his hair.

"You do your best to keep her comfortable and soothe her."

"I've been doing that all night."

"Then keep up the good work." She patted his arm. "And don't try to rush things. That'll only make 'em worse. Then how would you feel?"

He heaved a sigh. "I know you're right. But we've imposed on you and Audrey enough."

"Life happens." Her gaze narrowed. "And you're not imposing."

"I'm not so sure Audrey would agree with you."

Aunt Dee waved off the comment. "Nonsense. We all want what's best for Willow. And right now, that's for her to get well, and the only way she's gonna do that is for her little body to have the time and rest it needs to heal. We don't have any reservations on the books, so y'all can stay right here for as long as you need."

While he knew she was right... "In that case, the least I can do is pay you your nightly rate, just like any other guest."

She scowled, perching her fists on her denim-clad hips. "You most certainly will not. You're family, not a guest." Perhaps she ought to talk to Audrey, because Tyler was certain she did not feel the same way. "Now, I've got cattle to see to." She started toward the door. "Do yourself a favor and get some rest while that baby's sleepin', and I'll check in on you later."

Sleep? Not likely when he had so much on his mind. "I'll do my best."

Pulling the door open, she stepped onto the porch. "That was an order, not a suggestion." With a wink, she continued down the steps and to her truck.

With a wave, he closed the door as she drove away, then set his mug on the counter before checking on Willow. This was the longest she'd slept all night. So he continued to the sofa and made himself comfortable. Yet try as he might, he couldn't sleep for all the thoughts tumbling through his head. He had three months to start building a new life for him and Willow. But that wasn't easy to do when you had no clue as to what that life might look like.

As a former real estate agent, he'd worked with countless clients looking for the perfect home to raise a family. One with desirable schools and a good-sized yard where their kids could play. But he'd never contemplated anything like that for himself. Not even when he and Audrey had purchased their house. Back then the only things he'd focused on were that the rundown historic home had potential, and they were able to get it way below market price.

He stared into the cabin's ancient rafters. *God, show me what I'm supposed to do.*

Yet while he'd hoped for some sort of epiphany, his eyelids grew heavy instead. He felt himself drifting, until he was jolted awake by Willow's pathetic cries.

After a frenzied diaper change, he offered her a bottle, but she batted it away, crying harder. And he still had another thirty minutes before her next round of fever reducer.

Wearing a path around the sofa, he moved her from the crook of his arm to his shoulder, patting and rubbing her back. "I know, Willow. I'm sorry you feel bad." *God, I'm doing everything I know to do. Help me. Please.*

A loud knock at the door had him turning that way, wondering if Aunt Dee was checking on him again. At this point, he'd welcome whatever help he could get.

He yanked the door open, and the sight of Audrey standing on the other side looking nothing less than gorgeous in tan shorts and an off-white T-shirt, her long not-totally-blond-yet-not-quite-brown locks spilling past her shoulders, only amplified his incompetence.

Her concerned gaze moved from him to Willow and back. "May I?" She held out her hands.

"Please." Waving her inside, he handed off his niece, praying Audrey might be able to soothe the child. He closed the door as she wandered the space, then he collapsed onto the sofa, dropping his head in his hands. He hadn't felt this helpless since that day Audrey told him she wanted a divorce.

"Her fever's up," Audrey said behind him.

"I know that!" The words came out sharper than he'd intended. He shook his head and pushed to his feet to face her. "I'm sorry. She can't have the medicine for another ten minutes."

Nodding, she looked at Willow. "Then let's see if we can find a way to distract her until then." Audrey rounded the sofa, continuing toward the door. "Maybe a change of scenery will improve your mood." She opened the door, moved onto the porch and down the steps, patting Willow as she went.

He followed, pausing on the porch as a breeze rustled the leaves of the live oak arching over the front yard.

"Do you feel that?" Audrey smiled down at his niece, who'd suddenly quieted. "That's the wind, and it feels especially nice on warm days like this. Yes, it does."

Watching them, he couldn't help noticing how natural Audrey looked holding Willow. It was then he recognized something he'd either missed or chosen to ignore the past four years.

Audrey was meant to be a mother. No wonder grief over the miscarriage had consumed her. Yet he hadn't realized it until just now. And it shamed him.

Approaching the porch with Willow nestled in one arm, Audrey eyed him. "You're looking pretty ragged this morning. How much sleep did you get?"

He dragged his fingers through his hair. "An hour or two."

"That much, huh?" Grinning, she glanced down at the now-quiet baby. "Based on the way your hair is standing on end, I'd have thought less than that."

Good to know his ineptitude was on full display.

Her shoulders rose as she took a deep breath. She met his gaze. "You can probably give Willow her fever reducer now. Then I'll take her back home with me so you can catch up on your beauty sleep."

Sighing, he shook his head. "I don't need your sympathy, Audrey."

She glared at him. "That's good, because it's not you I feel sorry for. But you can't give Willow the kind of care she deserves if you're not at your best. And since I'm planning to hang around the house anyway, I might as well take her while you get some much-needed rest."

Noting the six-seater utility vehicle parked alongside his truck, he said, "You planning to strap her car seat into that thing?"

"Why not? This is a ranch, not the interstate."

He'd never been a fan of humble pie. Now, as he choked down the hefty portion Audrey had served him, he lifted his chin a notch. "Let me gather her things."

Chapter Three

Audrey sat at the kitchen table in the ranch house just before three that afternoon, scouring the internet for the perfect accessories for the bunkhouse, while Willow slept atop a blanket pallet in the adjoining family room. She had never seen Tyler so beaten down and defeated. Not even when she'd lost their baby. Yet this morning, he'd looked positively exhausted. His bloodshot eyes were rimmed with dark circles. And he must've run his fingers through his hair hundreds of times for it to stick straight up like that.

Yet despite his miserable state, Audrey refused to feel sorry for him. He wasn't worthy of her sympathy.

Willow, on the other hand...

At least when Audrey's mother died, she and her sisters had Aunt Dee to step in. She'd sacrificed her life here at the ranch and moved to Houston to raise her nieces. But Willow had no one. No one but an uncle who knew nothing about babies. Yet he seemed determined to do right by his niece.

Though Audrey wouldn't tell Tyler for fear of making him feel as though he'd done something wrong, Willow had been about as perfect as a baby could be for her. She'd napped for a solid two hours. Then, after devouring a bottle, she drifted off again, allowing Audrey plenty of time to shop as well as make some updates to the new Web site she'd set up for the ranch and create a page for the forthcoming tent cabins. Though it wouldn't be live until the cabins were built, finished out and furnished. And at the rate Dirk, Tessa's fiancé, was going, Audrey wasn't sure how soon that would be.

While he'd planned to start on them once he'd finished transforming the ranch's old bunkhouse into a country getaway, the decision to turn the old barn into a venue had sidetracked him as he delved into the intricacies of that project. Thankfully, he'd also been looking to take on some help. Because while Dirk was good at what he did, he could only do so much on his own.

Hearing the door to the carriage porch open in the laundry room, Audrey turned to find Nash moseying toward her while her aunt paused to remove her boots. Audrey gave the aged dog a rub. When he spotted Willow sleeping in the next room, Audrey accompanied him into the tiled space. Continuing onto Aunt Dee's new Oriental rug in shades of brown, rust and blue, he paused to give Willow a quick sniff before plopping down beside the pallet and resting his chin atop his paws.

"Good boy, Nash." Audrey stroked his head.

"He always did like the little ones." Aunt Dee approached, her clothes dusty, her face covered in dirt and sweat. "He used to do the same thing when Tessa's boys were babies." She eyed Audrey's computer. "You doin' some work?"

She joined her aunt. "Just playing around with the Web site." And imagining herself juggling both a career and a child.

"That reminds me." Her aunt met her gaze. "Pastor called today. Seems they're wantin' to do somethin' other than our usual Christmas potluck to bring folks together durin' the holiday season and wondered about havin' some sort of event here at Legacy Ranch."

"What kind of event?"

"Well—" she scratched her head "—he mentioned a campfire, singin', eatin', that sorta stuff. I don't know that he's homed in on anything specific."

"Something outside, though?"

Dee's nod had ideas sparking in Audrey's mind.

"You know, this could be just what we need to get things going with the tent cabins."

"How so?" Her aunt watched her.

"We've talked about having a communal campfire area near the cabins. We could host it out there, maybe even let folks tour one of the cabins—assuming they're ready by then. Oh, and we might be able to get some photos that would look great on the Web site."

Her aunt's smile made her blue eyes sparkle. "I like the way you think, sister."

"I'll keep pondering. After all, a successful event will benefit everyone."

Willow whimpered and Nash stood, looking from the baby to Audrey and her aunt and back.

"You grab Willow." Aunt Dee started toward the utility sink in the laundry room. "Much as I'd like to cuddle her, I'm filthy."

While her aunt washed up, Audrey continued alongside the squirming bundle and knelt beside her. "Hello there, sweet girl. Did you have a good nap?"

The baby looked up at her and cooed, melting Audrey's heart.

She scooped the child into her arms and stood, savoring that sweet baby scent. "Are you feeling better?"

"Aw, looky there." Wiping her hands, Aunt Dee spoke over Audrey's shoulder. "She's smilin'."

"I think you're right." Audrey pressed her cheek against the baby's head. "Her fever's definitely down." And while Audrey would be sad to see Willow go, she was looking forward to being rid of Tyler and settling into her new life here at Legacy Ranch. One that would, hopefully, include her own child.

A loud knock came from the front door.

Audrey eyed her aunt. "Would you mind getting that while I check her diaper, please? It might be Tyler." Returning to the family room, she retrieved a changing pad, diaper and wipes from Willow's bag before laying her down. Audrey unfurled the swaddling blanket before unsnapping Willow's purple romper adorned with pink and blue butterflies.

"You sure you got enough sleep?" she heard her aunt say as she approached the kitchen from the entry hall a short time later. "Cuz those eyes of yours are tellin' a diff'rent story."

"Yes, ma'am," Tyler replied. "Though I'm sure I'll sleep good in my own bed tonight."

Audrey was snapping Willow's outfit back into place when Aunt Dee and Tyler appeared.

"Your *own* bed?" Her aunt scowled.

Audrey lifted the baby into her arms. "Guess who's feeling better?" She glimpsed Tyler then. Whatever sleep he'd gotten hadn't done him much good. Wearing jeans and a heather-gray T-shirt, he looked even more haggard than he had this morning, except for his hair being combed.

Turning her way, he all but froze. Then just stared.

"Are you okay?" Still holding Willow, she eyed him as she stood.

With a jerk of his head, he cleared his throat. "Yeah. I, uh, I'm just glad she's improving." He stepped closer. "She looks happier."

"Her fever is down." Audrey eyed the bundle in the crook of her arm. "We just need to pray it stays that way."

"For sure," he said. "I'd hate for her to relapse on the drive home."

"Speakin' of that." Aunt Dee planted a fist on each hip, looking from Audrey to Tyler. "Just cuz Willow's fever broke doesn't mean she's outta the woods. It could spike again just as soon as the fever reducer wears off." She inched closer to Tyler, visually scrutinizing him. "Besides that, you look like death warmed over. Far as I'm concerned, sendin' that baby on a road trip with you would be child abuse."

Tyler's mouth dropped open. "I—"

"Y'all get a good night's sleep at the cabin then hit the road first thing tomorrow mornin'." She jerked a thumb toward Willow. "Assumin' little bit here doesn't regress."

"We're ho-ome!" Audrey's six-year-old nephew, Bryce, hollered from the entry hall.

Seconds later, the brown-haired boy bounded into the kitchen, followed by his auburn-haired older brother, Grayson, and mom, Tessa.

"What's going on?" Tucking her short brown waves behind an ear, Tessa eyed each of the adults. "How's Willow?"

"Her fever's gone," said Audrey.

"*For now*," Aunt Dee added.

Moving alongside Audrey, Tessa palmed the baby's head. "Let's pray it's down for good." Her gaze moved from Audrey to Tyler. "May I hold her?"

He nodded. "Be my guest."

Tessa smiled as Audrey passed her the infant. "It seems like ages since my boys were this small."

Aunt Dee eyed her great-nephews. "You boys grab you a snack." Her attention shifted to Tyler. "Have you eaten anything?"

"No, ma'am. But I'm not hungry."

She glared at him. "Tyler Caldwell, don't you go fibbin' me."

Sending Audrey a wide-eyed look, he responded, "Um, a bowl of cereal might be good."

"I got some bacon leftover from breakfast. How 'bout a BLT?"

The corners of his mouth attempted some semblance of a smile. "That sounds good, too."

"Heavy on the mayo, right?"

He smiled in earnest then. "You remembered that?"

Glancing over her shoulder, Audrey's aunt lifted a blond brow. "You'd be surprised what I remember."

In no time, she handed Tyler the sandwich. He sat down at the table and, for someone who supposedly wasn't hungry, he devoured his food mighty fast.

"Alright, boys." Tessa handed Willow back to Audrey. "Homework time."

"But I don't have any homework." Bryce frowned.

"You have a spelling test to study for."

"Aww." The kid slouched.

"Come on." She coaxed both boys out of the kitchen and upstairs.

Meanwhile, Aunt Dee eyed Audrey. "Why don't you take Tyler and Willow for a little ride on the UTV. The three of you have been cooped up all day. Some fresh air'll do you good."

While Audrey was more than happy to go for a ride around the ranch, she was getting annoyed with her aunt's attempts to force her and Tyler together.

"It's one of those rare days with moderate temps and low humidity. The kind you don't want to waste bein' cooped up inside," her aunt added.

"It did feel pretty good out there," said Tyler.

"See." Aunt Dee turned an innocent look toward Audrey. "You can show him what all's goin' on around the ranch."

Audrey willed herself to remain calm. *Just one more day. You can do this.*

"I guess a little fresh air would be nice." She turned her attention to Tyler. "What do you think?"

He stood. "I'm ready when you are."

Approaching him, she said, "Then if you'll take Willow, you can head out front to the utility vehicle and I'll be right behind you." She transferred Willow to his arms, trying to ignore his masculine scent that still lived in her memory.

When he disappeared out the front door, she approached her aunt.

"Stop trying to push me and Tyler together. There's nothing left between us. Whatever we had died long ago." *Right along with our baby.*

Aunt Dee frowned. "I'm just tryin' to get the poor fella to relax. He's wound up tighter'n a two-dollar watch. Besides, just 'cause the two of you are no longer married doesn't mean I stopped carin' about him. That boy has always held a special place in my heart." Glaring at Audrey, she huffed a sigh. "Why can't the two of you just be friends?"

Because Tyler had been emotionally unavailable when Audrey needed him most. But she couldn't tell Aunt Dee that because Audrey had never told her family she was pregnant. So she turned on her heel and continued toward the door.

Audrey hated him. Tyler could tell by the rigid set of her shoulders and her pulsating jaw as she drove him and Willow around the ranch yesterday. So despite his eagerness to learn more about the changes taking place at Legacy Ranch, he'd kept his questions to himself over supper with her family, then brought Willow back to the cabin as soon as the meal ended, claiming he needed to get her to bed early since they'd be leaving today.

It wasn't a lie, though he would've preferred to hang around and learn more about their plans for the old barn and something they referred to as tent cabins. But what they'd done to the bunkhouse—which hadn't been much more than a dilapidated shack the last time he saw it—was pretty remarkable. On their drive yesterday, Audrey had shown him the one-room structure that had been transformed into a relaxing country getaway for families.

Now, as he sat in the rocking chair on the log cabin's front porch the next morning, nursing his second cup of coffee while Willow slept inside, he felt as though someone had set an anvil on his chest. He wished he had more time to show Audrey he'd changed. That while he still struggled to open his heart completely, he wasn't the same man who'd let her walk out of his life without a fight. That through God's gift of Jesus, he'd been transformed. Not entirely, but he was definitely a work in progress.

Wearing a T-shirt and jeans, he inhaled a hefty dose of morning air. Though it was far from crisp, the humidity was low enough to make seventy-two feel almost cool. He savored the sounds of cattle lowing in the pasture and birds chirping somewhere in the live oak canopy. Not to mention the traffic noise that was noticeably absent.

That alone had him envying Audrey and Tessa. The ability to escape the city and start over in the country where you could hear yourself think. That was exactly what he needed. But with Willow being sick, he hadn't been able to concentrate on much else, let alone relax. And now that she was better, it was time to head back to Fort Worth and start making some decisions about their future.

Downing the last of his coffee, he lifted his gaze to the cloudless blue sky. *God, I've got nothing. Not a clue as to what a life with Willow should look like. I want to do right by her. I'm willing to go anywhere and do anything, so long as You're leading me. Please, don't let me mess things up this time.*

Hearing Willow's whimper through the door he'd left slightly ajar, he stood and started that way in his bare feet. "I'm coming, princess." He deposited his mug on the counter beside the door as he entered, then continued across the wooden floor to the portable crib positioned behind the sofa.

When Willow spotted him, her fussing stopped. Her eyes fixed on him, she grew more animated, wiggling and moving her mouth as though she had something to say.

Smiling, he picked her up and nestled her in

the crook of his arm, thanking God she was well again. "I'm glad you're feeling better." Listening to her cry, not knowing how to ease her discomfort had been the worst thing ever. "You're probably ready for some breakfast, aren't you?"

After changing her diaper, he fixed a bottle before returning to the porch. As he settled into the rocker again, he heard a vehicle approaching. Soon, Aunt Dee's twenty-some-year-old blue Chevy truck appeared. With the window rolled down, she rested an elbow on the sill and waved before easing to a stop beside his pickup.

Seconds later, she stepped out of the vehicle, Nash bounding out behind her. "How's our girl doin' this mornin'?" She started his way.

"Much better. Save for a 3:00 a.m. feeding, we both slept through the night."

"Glad to hear it." Wearing her usual jeans, chambray shirt and boots, she continued onto the porch, nudging the brim of her straw cowboy hat back a notch, while Nash explored the yard. Beside Tyler, she smoothed a tanned hand over Willow's downy hair. "Too bad y'all can't hang around a while longer. Give you a chance to relax and enjoy the ranch."

He glanced up at her. "I think we both know that wouldn't sit well with Audrey."

Lowering her hand, the woman sighed. "I s'pose. For what it's worth, I've enjoyed havin' you here. You've always held a special place in my heart, Tyler. I've missed you."

Warmth oozed through his core. "I've missed you, too." He liked her no-nonsense approach to life. Aunt Dee was one of those rare people who was comfortable with who she was. Never hostile or self-serving, but she wasn't afraid to speak her mind.

He set the bottle aside and moved Willow to his shoulder.

"What time you plannin' to head out?"

"As soon as we're packed up." Though he'd need to see Audrey one last time and have her sign that listing agreement. In all the chaos of Willow getting sick, he'd almost forgotten about it.

"In that case, I'll say my goodbyes now."

He stood. "You want to hold Willow?"

Grinning, she said, "Thought you'd never ask." She took the infant into her arms. "Sweet baby. You be a good girl for Tyler. No more gettin' sick, ya hear me?"

Though it might have been his imagination, he was pretty sure Willow nodded. Even she knew not to argue with Aunt Dee.

After a few more moments, she kissed Willow's cheek and passed her back to him. "You take care, Tyler." Her blue eyes bore into him. "And please, stay in touch."

Wrapping his free arm around her shoulders,

he pulled her close, wondering how Audrey would feel about that. "I'll do my best."

She stepped off the porch to continue across the grass. "Come on, Nash."

The dog took off after her. And as he returned to the rocker, they pulled away, leaving him with Willow and his thoughts. Until the sound of another vehicle caught his attention.

He watched as Audrey rolled around the bend in the UTV.

His muscles tightened. What was she doing here?

She eased the vehicle to a stop and killed the engine before slipping out of her seat to head toward him. Wearing a plain white T-shirt, tattered skinny jeans and sneakers, her long ponytail swaying with each step, she looked like a teenager. Though the image that had made it difficult for him to fall asleep last night was the one of her holding Willow yesterday. She'd looked so natural. And for perhaps the first time, he realized what the miscarriage had taken from her. From them.

Dragging a hand over his face, he looked away. "I hope the two of you slept well last night."

Of course she had. Because it meant she'd soon be rid of him.

He finally met her gaze as she neared the porch. "Yes. We're both doing much better this morning."

She gave a single nod. "I'm glad to hear it." Looking everywhere but at him, she said, "So Tessa and I were talking last night." Hands in her back pockets, Audrey ran the toe of her sneaker over the grass. "The decision to move ahead with turning the old barn into a venue has consumed more of Dirk's time than he—*we*—had anticipated. That's impacted the timeline on the tent cabins."

Audrey had shown him the sites for those on their drive yesterday. Said that while the structures would be very tent-like with a canvas canopy tarp roof and sides, they'd also be air-conditioned and heated. Perched atop a wooden platform, they'd offer the ultimate glamping experience.

"Before we can do anything, the platforms need to be built." She eyed him now. "That's where you come in."

"Me?" Since when was he part of the equation? "I'm not following you."

She eyed Willow. "May I hold her?"

"Sure." He stood as she joined him on the porch, then transferred his niece to Audrey's waiting arms, noticing her instantaneous smile.

"Hello, sweet girl." Patting Willow's bottom, she turned her attention back to him. "In the words of Aunt Dee, you're wound up tighter than a two-dollar watch."

Dragging his fingers through his hair, he

chuckled. "She always did have a way with words."

"Yes, she does." She glanced at Willow then back to him. "She wasn't wrong, though. I've never seen you like this. You were always so confident. Or pretended to be, anyway. This situation with Carrie and Willow has knocked you off your game. You're in unfamiliar territory and you're terrified of messing up."

His gaze darted to hers. And the way she looked at him—studied him—had him feeling exposed.

Suddenly uncomfortable, he said, "What does that have to do with the tent cabins?"

"We're going to be hosting a holiday event for the church, complete with a campfire in the area where the tent cabins will be. As soon as Aunt Dee told me, I knew I wanted those cabins built, furnished and ready to go. After all, word of mouth is the best advertising." Swaying Willow back and forth, Audrey took a deep breath. "So, I have a proposition for you."

He narrowed his gaze, clueless as to where she might be going with this.

"Since you're on a leave of absence, rather than hurrying back to Fort Worth, perhaps you'd be interested in building the pier and beam platforms for the cabins. The manual labor might alleviate some of your stress so you can take a levelheaded approach to all of those decisions you need to make."

Even after all these years, the woman could still read him. And he found that both comforting and unnerving. Still, ever since he saw how Aunt Dee had breathed new life into this log cabin and the once-forsaken bunkhouse, he'd been itching to strap on a tool belt. However—

"I thought you were eager to get rid of me."

Pink tinged her cheeks. "I'm more eager to get going on those tent cabins. And I know from working with you on our house that A—you're capable of anything—and B—how detailed you are in your work."

And he'd come a long way since then. "What about Willow?"

She hiked her chin a notch. "I'll watch her."

"What about *your* work?"

"I'm capable of handling both. At this point, a lot of it is computer work and shopping." She cocked her head. "So what do you say?"

A hearty yes was on the tip of his tongue. But life wasn't about his desires anymore. He had Willow to consider. And above all, what did God want him to do? Still, every time he thought about going back to Fort Worth, his muscles knotted, and his stomach clenched. Perhaps staying here a while longer would give him the clarity he needed. The manual labor and doing something to help Aunt Dee was also enticing.

He peered into the tree limbs. *God, what do You say? Should I stay? At least for a while?*

The rustling of leaves in the sudden breeze was all the confirmation he needed.

He met Audrey's gaze. "Have you run this idea past Aunt Dee and Dirk?"

"Not yet. I didn't want to get their hopes up until I talked to you."

"In that case, if they're in agreement, I'll do it."

"Good. Oh—" she pulled an envelope from her back pocket and handed it to him "—I thought you might need this."

"What is it?"

"The listing agreement. Signed and ready to go."

Chapter Four

Audrey pulled her white RAV4 into the parking lot of Hope Crossing Bible Church Sunday morning with Aunt Dee in the passenger seat, never dreaming she'd be excited her ex-husband had decided to remain at the ranch for a couple more weeks. Funny what the right motivation will do.

Aunt Dee and Dirk had concurred that it would be good to get the tent cabins going while the weather was still nice, allowing Dirk to work out the logistics of transforming the old barn into a venue. So after going over the plans for the tent cabins on Thursday, Dirk and Tyler set the posts for the four initial cabins on Friday. That alone was enough to have Tyler deciding to return to Fort Worth for his own tools, not to mention clothing and other belongings for himself and Willow. Yet while he'd planned to go Saturday and come back today, after Audrey offered to keep Willow, he'd made the round trip in a single day. Something that still surprised her.

Aunt Dee grabbed her Bible as Audrey shifted

into Park. "I sure wish Tyler would've come with us." Her aunt had extended the invite when he picked up Willow just before eight last night, though he'd politely declined. "I s'pose he's worn out after all that drivin' yesterday."

That and the fact that Tyler wasn't a church-going kind of guy. The only time they'd ever attended during their marriage was when they visited Aunt Dee. They hadn't even gotten married in a church. Instead, after she'd accepted his impromptu proposal, they'd opted for a wedding chapel in Lake Tahoe, much to the chagrin of her family.

Though Audrey had been brought up in church, she'd turned her back on the whole notion of religion as soon as she went off to college in Dallas. And she'd not given it another thought until after her divorce. Her miscarriage had left her feeling so hollow that she'd longed for something to fill that void. Then one of her coworkers invited her to a Bible study. Audrey agreed, and the next thing she knew she was attending Sunday morning worship, too. While her teenage self may have thought church boring, she suddenly found herself captivated by the Bible's stories of ordinary people who'd overcome impossible circumstances with God's help. And she wanted to be one of those people.

God may not have moved any mountains in her

life, but He was always with her and that made life better.

"Maybe." Audrey turned off the ignition before retrieving her purse and Bible and stepping into the pleasant morning air, wearing skinny jeans and a silky sleeveless white blouse over strappy high-heeled sandals.

"We may as well grab us a seat," said Aunt Dee. "Tessa and the boys are runnin' late, so we'd best save space for them."

Minutes later, they moved through the small foyer, pausing to greet a few people before continuing into the sanctuary with its padded pews and stained glass windows stretching along both sides. Surveying the space, Audrey spotted a familiar figure sitting at the end of a row to their left, a little more than halfway down the aisle. Her steps slowed, her gut clenching.

"Is that—?" Aunt Dee picked up her pace, the sleeves of her bright pink chiffon blouse fluttering with each step. "It *is* you!" She rested a hand atop Tyler's shoulder.

He stood then, his smile wide as he looked from her aunt to Audrey. "What are you two doing here?"

"What are we doin' here? This is *my* church," said Dee.

"I thought you went to that little white clapboard one out in the country."

Her aunt waved a hand. "It closed its doors

three years ago, so I've been comin' here since. Don't know why I didn't do it sooner, though, since I know most of the congregation." Perching a hand on her hip, she eyed Tyler. "Had you been plannin' to come here all along?"

"Yes, ma'am." He glanced Audrey's way. "I didn't want to interfere with your routine."

Interfere? How about throwing her for a loop? Since when did Tyler go to church?

"Psh." Her aunt waved a hand. "You ought to know better'n that, Tyler."

Gathering her wits, Audrey finally met his gaze. "Where's Willow?"

"In the nursery." He smiled then. "The way the two workers were oohing and aahing over her, I have no doubt she's in good hands." His gaze darted between Audrey and her aunt. "The pastor said they have connection classes after the service. Will the two of you be staying?"

Aunt Dee's brow puckered. "Connection classes?"

"That's what they call adult Sunday school now," said Audrey.

Her aunt looked at her as though she'd sprouted horns. "Since when?"

Audrey cleared her throat. "Never mind." She dared a glance Tyler's way. "And yes, we usually stay for connection classes." Though in a church this small, there was only one class designated for single adults. And just the thought of sitting in the same room for an hour with her ex-husband had her insides squirming. Perhaps she'd consider joining her aunt in the ladies' class today.

"Then you can meet us back at the house for lunch," her aunt tossed out. "Pot roast is in the oven and rolls are a risin'."

"I appreciate the offer, Aunt Dee, but I can't keep intruding on you for meals."

"Intruding? They're part of our deal. I promised you room and board, 'cept for breakfast. Now, if you don't want to dine with us, then just let me know and I'll fix up a plate you can eat at the log cabin."

The piano began to play.

Aunt Dee nodded toward the pew. "Mind if we join you?"

"Not at all." Stepping into the aisle, he motioned for them to take a seat.

"Tessa and her crew will be here shortly," Dee said as Audrey slipped into the row. "So scoot on down so there'll be room for them." Then—to Audrey's surprise—her aunt sat down next to Tyler. And by the time Tessa, her boys and Dirk joined them, Audrey and Tyler were on opposite ends of the pew. And that suited Audrey just fine.

Connection class couldn't have been more awkward, though. Audrey should've gone with Aunt Dee, but instead she'd let Tessa talk her into going with her and Dirk—and Tyler.

When Tyler introduced himself, the teacher promptly asked if he and Audrey were related.

"Uh, yes." Tyler dragged a hand over his hair. "We...used to be married."

To his credit, the teacher never missed a beat. He simply welcomed Tyler and proceeded as though it was no big deal. But by the time lunch was over, Audrey needed a break. So while Tyler and Willow headed back to the log cabin, she changed clothes then took off for Brenham, still trying to grasp the fact that Tyler had gone to church of his own volition. Meanwhile, *he* probably thought she was only there because of Aunt Dee.

And why does that matter?

Because she'd changed. She didn't go to church for show or to please someone else, but because she had a personal relationship with Jesus Christ and wanted to grow in her knowledge of Him.

What if Tyler was there for the same reason?

Her knuckles grew white atop the steering wheel. Everyone needed Jesus. So she couldn't begrudge Tyler. But forgiving him was another matter.

She pulled into the supercenter's crowded parking lot. Not only was she in need of some toiletries, the store was likely to have their Christmas decor out, too, and she wanted to see what they had.

This year, there'd be a lot more decorating

around the ranch, starting with the entrance. After all, you only have one opportunity to make a first impression, and she wanted it to be extra special with lights and evergreen garlands.

Her excitement was building by the time she walked through the store's automatic doors. She grabbed a cart and perused the personal care aisles before making her way to the garden center that had been transformed into a winter wonderland with a large display of trees and aisle after aisle of lights, decorations and wrappings.

She inched up and down the rows, scrutinizing each and every item. And by the time she was finished, her cart was brimming with artificial evergreen wreaths and garlands, along with multiple spools of red ribbon and boxes of little white lights. Because while Aunt Dee had decorations dating all the way back to the 1940s, most of her decorating was relegated to inside the house and its front porch.

Humming a Christmas carol, Audrey started toward the grocery section at the opposite end of the store for the short list of items Aunt Dee had sent with her, though she was soon sidetracked by some adorable infant outfits that would be perfect for Willow. After all, as the weather grew cooler, she'd need her little legs covered.

Audrey picked up a tiny pair of leopard-print leggings that were beyond cute paired with the tan-colored onesie boasting a pair of leopard-print hearts outlined in pink. She thumbed through the stack, noting the sizes.

"Audrey?"

Looking up, she found Tyler standing a couple feet from her, hands atop a grocery cart that held Willow's car seat. "Tyler." She inched toward him, just enough to peer past the car seat's canopy and glimpse a wide-eyed Willow. Audrey couldn't help smiling. "It appears she likes shopping."

His smile was tentative. "You caught her on a good day."

Returning her attention to his niece, she said, "I was just checking out a few items for you." She glanced Tyler's way. "Does she have many fall and winter clothes?"

He shook his head. "Just sleepers and onesies."

"Oh, we can't have that." She focused on Willow. "No. You need a little style in your wardrobe, don't you, sweet girl?"

The baby's tiny legs began to kick.

"See, she agrees." Audrey held up the items in her hands. "What do you think about this?"

"Leopard print?"

"Yes. It'll look adorable with her dark hair." Returning to the display, she motioned for Tyler to follow. "But they've got lots of other stuff, too, and they're relatively inexpensive, which is good since she'll outgrow them quickly." She continued to peruse the selection, the irony of shopping for baby clothes with Tyler not lost on her.

He moved beside her. "About church. I'm sorry, I know it was awkward. I'll find another house of worship to attend next week."

With a country tune spilling from the speakers overhead, she tilted her head. "How long have you been going to church?"

He shrugged, thumbing through a stack of shirts. "Shortly after our divorce, I guess."

She considered him for a moment, recalling the seemingly well-used Bible she'd noticed him carrying this morning. "Interesting. Me, too."

He did a double take, his gaze suddenly searching hers, though she couldn't decide if it held curiosity or skepticism. Probably not so different from her own expression.

Continuing to riffle through the infant clothes, she said, "You know, there aren't a lot of churches in close proximity to Legacy Ranch. And since you'll only be here a couple more weeks—" she shrugged and looked him in the eye "—don't worry about finding another church. I can handle it if you can."

His light brown eyes were wide. "You're sure?"

"Yes. Now, help me pick out some clothes for Willow."

No doubt about it. Tyler was out of shape. Lifting all that lumber on Monday had his muscles protesting when he woke up Tuesday morning. Things weren't much better this Wednesday morning, either. But he couldn't let that stop him when he had a job to do. So after popping a couple of over-the-counter pain relievers and dropping Willow off with Audrey, he returned to the area where the platforms for the tent cabins were being built. Though he had yet to complete the first one, it was almost there. He just needed to finish up the stairs to the front porch and back deck. One thing was for sure. When these things were finished, they were sure to be some of the fanciest tents he'd ever seen.

The canvas roof and walls would create a tent-like atmosphere, allowing folks to experience the sounds of nature and the pitter-patter of rain, all while enjoying the comforts of real beds, a bathroom, a kitchenette, even air-conditioning. Roughing it never sounded so good.

Now, as he packed up his tools Wednesday afternoon, he took in the view from the gentle rise where the platforms were being constructed. The same view guests would have from their private deck. Charolais grazed in the sun-drenched pasture beyond the creek below while cattle egrets wandered among them, sometimes perching atop their massive companions.

City dwellers would get a kick out of that.

What was he talking about? *He* was a city dweller.

In the shade of a post oak, he hoisted his air compressor into the truck bed, mentally commending Aunt Dee for choosing this site. The stretch of trees along the top of the rise had enough space for a cabin to be tucked between them, affording shade and allowing the structures to blend into the landscape.

Out of nowhere, an image of Audrey looking at baby clothes on Sunday played across his mind. Her acknowledgment that she, too, had started going to church after their split had come as a surprise. It also had him wondering, if they'd gone to church during their marriage, would they still be married?

He shook his head. Not if he hadn't changed. Opened himself, allowing her to see the real him, insecurities and all. But he'd thought they'd make him look weak. Still did, he supposed.

When I am weak, then I am strong.

Paul's words to the Corinthians challenged Tyler's opinion. But he shook it off, checking his watch. It was a little earlier than he'd knocked off the last two days, but at least it would give Audrey a break. Since he'd decided to have supper at the cabin tonight, she'd have time to tend to her own business without having to worry about Willow.

She's the one who suggested you stay.

Only to speed up things with the tent cabins. Not so she could hang out with him. Not that he wouldn't mind spending more time with her. Getting to know the woman she'd become. By the grace of God, he wasn't the same man who'd watched her walk out of his life. And now that he knew she'd been going to church, he suspected she'd changed, too.

His phone rang and he couldn't help smiling when he saw Reid's name on the screen. "Hey, buddy. Good to hear from you."

"Right back atcha, brother. And happy birthday."

Birthday? Tyler glanced at his watch, noting the date. "Thanks. I hadn't even paid attention." Was that why he'd been feeling so melancholy? He snorted. "Too bad I don't have more to show for the last thirty-five years."

"You own a successful business."

"Reid, you and I both know that's not important."

"The money may not be, but we provide well-built homes to folks at honest prices. *And* you have a precious little one who's been entrusted to your care."

"Willow got the raw end of that deal."

"Stop being so hard on yourself, Ty. You're part of God's plan for Willow's life. Yes, it's a shame her mama is gone, but that wasn't a surprise to God. You're the one she's going to look to for guidance as she grows. Don't shun that. Embrace it for the gift that it is."

A gift? One he didn't deserve. "She has forced me to slow down and rethink my life. Not that I've come to any conclusions."

"You will, Tyler. Keep praying and trusting God. He'll let you know in His timing."

Tyler rubbed the back of his neck. "I'm trying. It's not easy, though."

The sound of a vehicle had him turning as Dirk's truck approached.

"I need to let you go, Reid."

"Alright, brother. Have a good one."

Dirk's truck rolled to a stop beneath a nearby tree. Moments later, he emerged, followed by his service dog, Molly, a pretty black-and-white border collie.

"How's it going?" The man with blond hair and a beard approached.

"Slow, but steady."

Moving past Tyler, Dirk surveyed the progress. "For a one-man job, I'd say you're doing good. Wish I could say the same."

Tyler approached him. "Problem?"

Hands on his hips, Dirk sighed. "I finally heard from the fellow I was looking at to lift the barn. The same guy who did my place." He'd shown Tyler some photos of an old barn on his parents' property that he'd transformed into a combo home and woodworking shop. "Unfortunately, he's booked for a minimum of six months."

Tyler let go a low whistle. "That long, huh?

Audrey won't be happy about that." He picked up his tool bag and set it in the truck bed.

"Me neither." Dirk sighed.

"You know anyone else who could do the job?"

Shaking his head, Dirk said, "I'll have to do some research. See if I can locate another company."

Tyler rubbed the scruff on his chin, eyeing the cattle once again. "Well, if you're interested, I know a guy." Facing Dirk, he continued. "He's out of Johnson County, south of Fort Worth. Specializes in all aspects of timber-framed structures. Deconstruction. Rebuilding. Restoration. He can barn jack with the best of them."

Dirk's brow arched. "You're familiar with his work then?"

"Enough to know he's a stickler for detail."

The rigid set of Dirk's shoulders eased. "In that case, I'm definitely interested."

Tyler nodded. "Alright, I'll give him a call tomorrow and see what he has to say."

"Great. I appreciate it." Dirk glanced toward the wood platform Tyler hoped to complete tomorrow. "Keep up the good work. And let me know if you need any help."

"Will do."

As Dirk drove away, Tyler finished loading his tools and was closing the tailgate when his phone rang. When he saw Audrey's name, his thoughts immediately went to Willow.

"Hey, Audrey. Everything okay?"

"Yes, of course. I'm just calling to suggest you go ahead and get cleaned up at the cabin before coming by the house for supper."

The last couple of days he'd picked up Willow first, then spent some time with her at the cabin before joining everyone else at the old farmhouse for supper. "I was thinking I'd just eat at the cabin tonight. I'm kind of tired."

"Oh."

Was he imagining the disappointment in her tone?

"Are you sure?" she continued. "Aunt Dee is grilling steaks."

His mouth began to water. Aunt Dee's steaks were better than those from some of the finest steakhouses. Not only did she know how to cook them so they were tender and moist, her secret seasoning was beyond perfection.

"Ooo...that's an offer that's too good to refuse."

"I thought so. Get yourself cleaned up, relax a while and we'll see you about 6:30."

"What about Willow?"

"She'll be fine here. She's asleep anyway." Audrey was being unusually accommodating.

Nonetheless, he headed back to the cabin and, after an extralong shower, propped his feet up in front of the television. Looked like they were in for some rain next week. Cooler temps too. Sweet.

When a commercial came on, he turned off the television and stared into the cabin's ancient rafters. He was thirty-five years old today. And what did he have to show for it? A failed marriage. No family, except for Willow.

He still found it almost laughable that she belonged to him. That he was responsible for her well-being. For raising her to be a godly, well-adjusted woman. Not messed up like the rest of his family. Including himself.

At least he had God to lean into. Without Him, neither Tyler nor Willow stood a chance.

"God, help me be the man You've called me to be."

Noting the time, he stood and grabbed his keys before heading outside to his truck. He really didn't feel like being around a bunch of people tonight. Even if it did mean a great steak dinner.

Still, he rolled up to the ranch house minutes later and parked alongside Dirk's pickup, thankful to have another male around. Back when Tyler and Audrey were married, it had been just him, the lone male against all five of the Hunt women, save for the rare occasion when Audrey's father had joined them. He felt for Dirk.

The sun hovered in the western sky as he stepped out of his truck. Then he noticed Tessa's boys on the porch, though the younger of the two promptly disappeared into the house, then reappeared seconds later.

"What's up fellas?" He started up the old brick walkway.

"Nothin'," said nine-year-old Grayson.

His six-year-old brother echoed him.

Their grins suggested they might be up to something, though he couldn't imagine what. "How was school?"

"Good," they responded simultaneously.

Then Tyler heard Willow crying inside the house. "Uh-oh. Sounds like Willow's upset."

Audrey pushed through the door, his red-faced niece screeching over her shoulder.

He promptly joined her on the porch and reached for Willow. Cradling her in the crook of his arm, he said, "What's the problem, sweetheart?" He patted her bottom. "What's got you so upset?"

Quieting, she stared up at him. A moment later, she smiled, melting his heart.

Audrey peered at the now-content child. "Oh, sure. Now she's happy." Her gaze darted to Tyler's. "I guess she was missing you."

"Me? Why would she miss me?"

Audrey's smile evaporated. "Duh. As far as she's concerned, you're her daddy. She relies on you to care for her and meet her needs." Her tone softened. "She loves you."

Were babies capable of loving?

Looking into Willow's contented face, he wanted to believe it. Because he suddenly realized how much he loved her. This tiny person who could do nothing for herself had captured his heart and filled it with unconditional love. It was unlike anything he'd ever experienced before. Exhilarating and terrifying all at the same time.

He blinked away the sudden moisture clouding his vision. "And I love her."

"Can we eat now?" Grayson groaned.

Audrey ruffled his auburn hair. "Always thinking about your stomach." She reached for the door. "Come on."

Still holding Willow, Tyler followed her into the entry hall then turned left into the living room before making a right toward the voices coming from the adjacent dining room.

As he approached, Aunt Dee, Tessa, Dirk, Audrey and the boys started singing "Happy Birthday." Meanwhile, he stood there in stunned silence, blinking away even more dampness from his eyes.

Aunt Dee came alongside him as he spotted the cake in the middle of the dining table. She wound her arms around his waist. "Happy birthday, Tyler."

"I can't believe you remembered."

"Not a year's gone by that a reminder hasn't popped up on my phone. And I've prayed for you every time. This year, we get to celebrate together." Her words had his throat thickening. And looking into her faded blue eyes, he actually felt as though he mattered. Perhaps for the first time ever.

As his gaze shifted to the child in his arms, he vowed to do whatever it took to make sure Willow always felt important. And that she always knew she was loved.

Chapter Five

Audrey peered out the rain-streaked window the following Monday, yet all she could see was Tyler's stunned expression as they sang "Happy Birthday" to him. The utter amazement and childlike wonder on his face was unexpected. And five days later, it still tugged at her heart, no matter how many times she tried to dismiss it.

Tyler had always had swagger. Not in an arrogant way, yet he possessed a confidence that drew people to him. Had drawn her to him. Not bad for a guy who was raised by a single mother and, more often than not, left to care for his little sister while his mom worked countless hours to keep a roof over their heads. Yet he never seemed to let that or anything else get him down. Not even when she lost their baby.

She grew to hate him for that, despite her own culpability. Even after coming to faith in Jesus. Though, with Tyler out of her life, it rarely crossed her mind. Until he showed up on her doorstep with a baby, ripping that old wound wide open and dousing it with salt. Before she learned of Willow's plight.

Yet at his birthday celebration last week, she'd glimpsed a side of Tyler she'd never witnessed before. A vulnerability that threatened everything she thought she knew about him.

Thunder rumbled as she stepped away from the window and started toward the kitchen for another cup of coffee. Tessa and her boys were at school. The rain that had started overnight and showed no signs of letting up meant Tyler couldn't work, so Audrey didn't have to care for Willow. And given that they were calling for rain into, and maybe even beyond, tomorrow, there was no telling how long it would be before Tyler could resume work on the tent cabins.

Thankfully, the furnishings for the bunkhouse had been delivered Friday morning, so she'd spent part of that day and the weekend getting the place situated. Tessa and Aunt Dee helped her get everything staged, then they snapped photos, both inside and out, and uploaded them to the Web site so they could start taking bookings.

She refilled her cup and leaned against the counter, blowing on the steaming liquid as a forlorn Nash moseyed toward her. She rubbed his head. "Don't worry, buddy. Your mama will be back soon."

Her gaze drifted to the window over the sink. The sky seemed to grow darker by the minute. And Aunt Dee was out there somewhere, trying to locate a cow that was due to calve any time.

Audrey shuddered. Her aunt had to be the gutsiest person she'd ever known.

With Nash on her heels, she retrieved her iPad from the table before returning to the living room. Then she sank into one of two comfy blue-gray chairs that flanked the fireplace while Nash settled at her feet. She'd just opened her tablet when a gust of wind sent the crepe myrtles outside the window into a frenzy. Lightning flashed. Thunder crackled, making her shudder.

Lord, please protect Aunt Dee.

Her phone rang, the notification appearing on the tablet screen.

"Aunt Dee?" She could hear the rain pounding her aunt's truck. "Did you find the cow?"

"Yes. Her calf is fine."

The woman's lengthy pause had Audrey asking, "Why do I sense a 'but' coming?"

Her aunt sighed. "Mama didn't make it."

"Any idea why?"

"No. She's never had any problem in the past. No tellin' what went wrong. I need to git her calf up to the barn, but my truck's stuck in the mud and Gentry's off today." Gentry was her aunt's right-hand man around the ranch—though Audrey and her sisters suspected something more.

"Do you need me to come and help you?"

"I wish you could, Audrey, but I'm afraid that little vehicle of yours wouldn't be much help. I already called Tyler. I'm just lettin' you know he's going to be dropping Willow off with you."

Thunder rumbled again, vibrating the house.

"I think it might be best if I go down to the cabin. I'd hate for Willow to be out in this weather."

"Sounds good. I'll let him know."

Making her way into the entry hall, Audrey tucked her phone in the back pocket of her jeans. Then she yanked open the door to the coat closet beneath the stairs to snag her rain jacket before continuing into the laundry room where she traded her sneakers for rubber boots.

Nash gave her a woeful look.

"Sorry, fella." She petted his head. "You need to stay in here where it's dry." With that, she stepped outside and splashed through multiple puddles on the way to her vehicle. Her windshield wipers moved at a frenzied pace as she drove down the muddy road. Minutes later, she pulled the SUV as close to the cabin as she dared then killed the engine and darted onto the porch.

Tyler swung the door open before she could knock. "Thanks for coming."

"No problem." The aroma of coffee enveloped her as she pushed her hood back and stepped inside.

"Willow is napping." Tyler grabbed his keys from the kitchen counter beside the door. "And she'll probably want to eat when she wakes up. Formula's on the counter." He pointed.

"Good to know." Eyeing his T-shirt and jeans, she added, "You're going to get soaked out there."

"I've got rain gear in the truck." He poked a thumb toward the window and the pickup parked alongside one end of the porch.

"Ah. Good thinking. Now, you'd better get going. I'd hate for anyone to be out in this weather any longer than necessary."

Despite the grumbling thunder outside, Willow continued to sleep so Audrey parked herself on the sofa and tried to envision a general layout and decorations for Christmas Under the Stars, making notes on her phone. After talking with the pastor yesterday, she had a better idea of what she wanted to do for the event.

Eventually, she heard Willow stirring. The sweet sound made Audrey smile. Standing, she slid her phone into her pocket as she rounded the sofa to peer into the small crib where Willow wriggled beneath her blanket. "Hello there, sweet girl."

Willow smiled up at her, melting Audrey's heart.

She scooped the child into her arms. "Did you have a good nap?" Nearly two weeks with Willow had only solidified Audrey's desire to become a mother. Yet adoption could be a lengthy process, making her wonder if she should rethink her timeline. But with all the goings-on around the ranch, not to mention the holiday season that would be here before they knew it, she couldn't even consider it until the new year.

Eyeing Willow, she said, "Let's change your diaper and fix you a bottle."

By the time they settled into the side chair near the fireplace, the rain was coming down even harder. And the thunder and lightning only heightened Audrey's concern. Noting the time on her watch, she was shocked to discover Tyler had been gone for a good hour and a half.

For a moment, she contemplated texting him but decided that would only delay him more.

"I sure hope Tyler and Aunt Dee get back soon. They don't need to be out in this weather. No they don't." Yes, she was conversing with an infant, one-sided as it might be.

Ah, if only she were as calm as Willow. How long did it take to pull a truck out of the mud? In a thunderstorm? While looking after a newborn calf?

Evidently a lot longer than she expected. Because another hour passed without a word. And while she'd contemplated calling Tyler or her aunt, she'd managed to refrain, not wanting to interrupt them. Meanwhile, with every clap of thunder her concern heightened.

Willow began to fuss. Was she sensing Audrey's anxiety or getting sleepy again?

Finally, she saw headlights outside the window.

With Willow in her arms, she swung the front door wide as a raincoat-clad Tyler emerged from his truck to dash onto the covered porch.

He shrugged out of his Frogg Toggs before pulling off his mud-covered boots and joining her inside. "It's not fit for man nor beast out there."

"What took you so long?" The words came out sharper than she'd intended.

"A big ol' limb had fallen across the road, so I had to go back to the barn for a chainsaw." He dragged his fingers through his damp hair. "Which ended up being out of gas. However, I didn't figure that out until I was ready to use it. So I had to go back to the barn. Then it took a while to cut the limb. Thankfully, when I finally got to Aunt Dee, I was able to pull her truck right out. Then I followed her back to the barn in case she encountered any issues." Moving to the counter, he set to work on a cup of coffee. "Cute little calf, though. Muddy as it was."

Noting his mud-caked jeans and shirt, Audrey mumbled, "Looks like it wasn't the only one." When he faced her again, she said, "You could have called to let me know what was going on."

"I was busy making sure everything was handled so I could get back here."

"You were out in a storm—for *two and a half hours*."

"What can I say, it was a healthy tree limb. It took me forever to tackle it."

Her heart hammered in her chest. "And you couldn't have at least texted me an update?"

The aroma of coffee began to permeate the air. But even that didn't calm her.

"Alright. Point taken. I'm sorry." Huffing out a breath, he watched her, the corners of his mouth twitching.

"What?"

"You were worried about me."

"Of course I was worried." To the point of having heart palpitations, but she wasn't about to tell him that.

His charming grin grated on her already frazzled nerves.

"What are you smirking about?"

Retrieving the steaming drink, he said, "You still care about me."

She felt her jaw drop. The nerve of him. "Oh, get over yourself. I was worried for Willow." Strolling toward the fireplace, she moved the child to her shoulder. "I mean, if something happened to you, she'd—" Audrey clambered for an excuse "—she'd become a ward of the state. She'd have no one." Which was true, though she wasn't being one hundred percent truthful. She may have been a teensy bit worried about his safety.

His smile evaporated, the color draining from his face. "You're right." He set his cup on the counter. "I mean, Carrie just ran to the store. Yet she never came back." His panicked gaze sought out Audrey's. "We never know when something might happen. And if I—" Looking away, he dragged a hand over his still-damp face.

After a long moment, he looked her way again. "Audrey, if something happens to me, will you take care of Willow? As in, be her legal guardian?"

Suddenly Audrey wished she hadn't made such a big deal about him being gone so long. She patted Willow. "Why would you ask me that?"

"Because you care about her." He inched toward her. "Because I trust you to do right by her."

Audrey shook her head. "This is absurd. Once you return to Fort Worth, we'll probably never see each other again." She ignored the sudden pang in the vicinity of her heart. "I'll be a stranger to her."

"But you would love her. Just the way you've done for almost two weeks now."

Audrey looked away from the intensity of his gaze, knowing he was right. It bugged her that he could read her so well. She lifted her chin. "What if you remarry?"

He scoffed, shaking his head. "Then I'll have

the paperwork changed. But after losing my sister in the blink of an eye, this isn't something I can put off. I'm just glad you brought it to my attention." He closed the short distance remaining between them, smelling of gasoline and manure. "Please, Audrey. I need to know Willow will be taken care of." His pleading expression had her swallowing hard.

She turned away. "*Alright*, I'll agree on one condition."

"Name it."

"You go get cleaned up." She waved her free hand in front of her face. "You smell like you've been rolling around in the pasture."

"No, just holding a newborn calf who decided she needed to use the bathroom." His smile returned. "It was kind of exciting."

Exciting for him, maybe, but she'd just dug herself a hole she wasn't sure how to get out of.

Thanks to seven inches of rain over two and a half days, Tyler hadn't made much progress on the tent platforms this week. Things had been too wet and muddy to even attempt working until Friday. Even then, he hadn't accomplished much.

To his surprise, though, the delay hadn't bothered him. Instead, he enjoyed the extra time with Willow. Her tiny Cupid's bow pout could melt his heart faster than a popsicle in the July sun. And while he wished Carrie could be here to see her daughter, he was thankful for the gift he'd been given.

Since Audrey's miscarriage, he'd never given another thought to fatherhood. Then he suddenly had Willow, and it terrified him. But being here at Legacy Ranch, things didn't seem so overwhelming. Perhaps because he had Audrey and Aunt Dee to guide him and show him what he should and shouldn't do. Talking with Reid the other night, Tyler had realized that God may very well have orchestrated the last two and a half weeks to bring him to this point where he viewed Willow as a precious gift and not a burden. And he could honestly say he was in no hurry to return to Fort Worth.

The weather had him and Willow spending the bulk of their time at the cabin this week. When Willow slept—which was more often than not—he'd contacted his attorney, setting the wheels in motion to name Audrey as Willow's guardian in the event anything happened to him. Then he'd poured over the internet, researching homes, neighborhoods and schools in and around the Fort Worth area. He'd also gotten in touch with his business acquaintance regarding the barn here at Legacy Ranch. Bruce Hendricks suspected it should be a straightforward job but would need to take a look at it first. So Tyler had passed the info on to Dirk so he could give the man a call to set up a date and time.

The downtime had also created some much-needed separation between Tyler and Audrey. While he had no doubt she adored Willow, her feelings toward him were questionable. Not that he could blame her. He'd let her walk out of his life and end their marriage without the slightest fight.

Audrey was too good for him. He'd known it from the moment they met. But that hadn't stopped him from pursuing her, determined to be a man worthy of her love. And for a while, he'd succeeded. Until the miscarriage. She was heartbroken, much the way his mother had been after his father walked out. And there'd been nothing Tyler could do in either instance to make things better. So he'd shut down, abandoning Audrey the way his father had done with Tyler's mom. Oh, he may not have walked out of Audrey's life, but he'd checked out emotionally.

Shaking off the unwanted memories, he tossed the remains of his third cup of coffee into the sink, realizing that, despite the setbacks brought on by the rain, it had been a good week. For the first time in—well, longer than he could remember—he'd truly relaxed.

Now, with what looked like a gorgeous fall Saturday ahead of him, and with temperatures only making it into the low seventies, he was looking forward to taking Willow to the barn to check on Marshmallow, the calf Aunt Dee had rescued.

Though Audrey's aunt was emphatic about not naming her cattle, he couldn't help himself. Once the calf had been cleaned up, its pristine hide was as white as marshmallows.

He donned his well-worn Texas Rangers World Series Champs ball cap before retrieving a freshly diapered Willow from the crib, then tucked her into the sling Audrey had given him for his birthday. It had taken him a while to figure out how to wrap the length of stretchy fabric around his torso, but once he got the hang of it, he actually liked it. And when Willow smiled up at him, he suspected she did, too.

Stepping outside, he savored the pleasant midmorning air. Live oak leaves rustled overhead, sending specks of sunlight dancing over the ground. A perfect day for a walk. Then, perhaps, a trip to Brenham for a few groceries, diapers and formula before throwing open the windows at the cabin and enjoying some college football.

Gravel ground beneath his boots as he strolled up the dirt road that led to the ranch house. Before reaching the cattle guard, though, he veered left to continue along the drive leading to the large red and white monitor barn that sat just beyond the house. The doors of the large metal structure stood wide open on both ends. Outside, a big blue tractor was parked beneath the lean-to on the barn's left side while covered pens stretched along the right.

He headed toward the pens, glancing down at Willow. "You ready to see Marshmallow?" Pausing beside the metal pipe fence, he eyed the calf with a pink nose. "Hey there, little one."

As if recognizing his voice, the pint-size creature started toward him, its movements awkward.

Tyler reached through the fence to rub its furry head.

"Good morning."

He turned at Audrey's voice. "Hello."

Though she'd watched Willow yesterday, he'd kept to himself the rest of the week—save for a couple of suppers—in part because he didn't want to take Willow out in the rain, but also to create some distance between him and Audrey. Every time he thought about it, he wanted to kick himself for suggesting she still cared about him. Like she'd said, once he left, they'd probably never see each other again.

"Thought you'd be working at the bunkhouse." Though her aunt said the place was all set, Audrey had continued to tinker.

"I finished. And we have our first booking for next weekend."

"Congratulations."

Smiling, she continued toward him clad in skinny jeans and a brown T-shirt, her long hair piled on top of her head in one of those messy buns he found way too attractive. "Dirk said you talked with a guy about the barn."

"I did." He nodded. "No timeline yet, but at least we know he's able to do the job."

Audrey let out a little squeal and playfully clapped her hands. "Things are finally starting to come together."

"Yes, but before you get too excited, remember, it's a process."

"I know, but if we can get the slab poured before the holidays, we'll be able to hit the ground running in January."

He felt a twinge in the vicinity of his heart. Come January, he'd be back in Fort Worth. Back to work. Willow would be in daycare. And after his research this week, they might be moving into a new house, too. And for some reason, that didn't make him as happy as it should.

Probably just fear of the unknown.

"As I recall, you have plenty of things to keep you busy before then." Watching her, he smoothed a hand along Willow's back. "Like styling the tent cabins—once they're done, that is. Getting ready for Christmas Under the Stars."

Her brown eyes widened. "That reminds me. Do you remember that Christmas we decorated our house and the yard with thousands of lights, making it look like a winter wonderland?"

"Of course I remember. We won the grand prize from the homeowner's association." That was the one and only time they'd done it. By the following Christmas, Audrey was gone.

"I'd like to do something like that for Christmas Under the Stars, but I'm not sure I can pull it off. After all, you were the one who brought our vision to life." Looking suddenly shy, she toed at the dirt with her rubber boot. "So I was wondering if, maybe, I could talk you into helping me." She shrugged, her gaze meeting his. "I may be good at design, but you're a genius when it comes to execution, not to mention getting electricity to everything."

"I don't know about genius." His chest puffed a bit. "What do you have in mind?"

"I'm still pondering." Looking out over the cattle-dotted pasture, she worried her bottom lip. "I mean, we're talking about a blank slate. I've looked online, but that's about it. Mostly because I have no idea how to get electricity to everything."

"Well, if you're going to buy outdoor decorations and lights, now's the time to do it. Once we're into November, things will be picked over."

"You're right. I hadn't thought of that." Worry puckered her brow. "November is less than a week away. That means I need to get started now. Like, today." Wide eyes met his. "What should I get, though?"

He held up his hands. "Hey, this is your brainchild. You must have some ideas." Audrey was always brimming with ideas. She was the one who'd had the vision for their house when they'd bought the rundown place. And her creative marketing ideas were only part of what had made her a successful real estate agent.

"A few. Nothing specific, though. All I know is I want lots of lights. A few large-scale decorations, perhaps."

"Aren't there a couple of home improvement stores in Brenham?"

A cow bellowed in the distance.

"Yes."

"That would be a good place to start. They usually have things on display, so you can see how they look lit up."

"That's not a bad idea." She cocked her head, the breeze tossing a lock of hair around her face. "What are your plans for today?"

"A trip to Brenham. A little football." He shrugged.

Audrey arched a brow. "If I were to buy you lunch, could I talk you into accompanying me to the home improvement centers? Because while I may be good at envisioning the finished product, you're the one who lets me know if my ideas will actually work."

They'd made a good team. Life was good back when they were married. Until he allowed that life to slip through his fingers. He could've stopped it, if he'd been a better man. Instead, he lost the best thing he'd ever had.

Yet here they were. The least he could do was try to make amends.

"Lunch, huh?"

She nodded.

"Any good Mexican joints in Brenham?"

She smiled. "I think we can make that happen."

Chapter Six

Despite second-guessing her lunch offer the entire drive to Brenham, things hadn't been nearly as awkward as Audrey had feared. Having Willow with them had certainly helped. Then Tyler told her how he'd made the switch to construction from real estate and subsequently gone into business with a man Tyler referred to as his spiritual mentor. Add that to the list of things she never expected to hear from him.

Then she told him about her decision to step away from real estate and fully embrace her family's legacy at the ranch. Something her father had never done. On the contrary, he would've sold off the land if Aunt Dee would've allowed it. Thankfully, she hadn't—and Audrey couldn't be more thrilled with this new direction her aunt had decided to take things. All while keeping it a working cattle ranch.

"I know I mentioned Christmas Under the Stars, but I'd like to decorate other areas of the ranch, too. Like the main entrance and the house, as well as the log cabin and bunkhouse."

"What do you think about this lighted reindeer trio?"

Standing on the polished concrete floor of the home improvement center, she eyed the white metal and mesh buck, doe and fawn adorned with festive red bows. "I like them a lot. They'd be perfect in a rustic setting like the ranch. I like that Nativity scene, too." She pointed to the metal silhouette of Joseph, Mary and the baby Jesus. "And I think some of those meteor shower lights in a couple of the trees would be stellar for the Christmas event."

"Out there where you'll have minimal lighting, they would really stand out." He arched a brow. "You're not going to want to completely wrap any of the trees, are you?" The worried look on his face had her grinning.

"You mean like that Bartlett pear tree we had in our front yard?"

He nodded.

"That was the centerpiece of our design. People came from all over town to see it. However, the trees here will still have their leaves, so no, that is not part of my plans."

"Okay, good." He visibly relaxed.

"You know, as I recall, wrapping that tree was *your* idea."

Looking suddenly sheepish, he shrugged. "It was."

She perched a fist on her hip. "So why the grief?"

"Let's just say I never realized I was afraid of heights until I attempted that."

She bit her lip to hold back a snicker. "In that case, I'm glad we won."

Willow began to fuss in her stroller.

"Uh-oh." Audrey slid the diaper bag from her shoulder. "Sounds like somebody's hungry."

"That she does." Unbuckling his niece, he looked at Audrey. "I guess we're both becoming adept at understanding her."

"I believe that's called survival skills." She unzipped one of the compartments to retrieve the insulated bag holding a bottle of warm water, along with a packet of powdered formula. Then, while she mixed the formula, Tyler took Willow into his arms.

When Audrey looked at the two of them, she couldn't help smiling. Tyler had grown more comfortable with Willow. Now he looked as though he'd been taking care of babies all his life.

His gaze narrowed. "What are you grinning about?"

She turned away. "Nothing. Mind if I feed her?"

"Be my guest." He placed Willow into her waiting arms.

"How precious."

98 *Their Texas Christmas Redemption*

The female voice had them looking up as an older couple approached.

The smiling gray-haired woman nudged the tall, thin man beside her. "Remember those days when our kids were that little?"

"Barely," her husband responded. "Y'all enjoy this time. They grow up fast."

"Such a sweet family," the woman cooed, her gaze falling to Willow. "She favors her daddy."

Audrey expected Tyler to correct the woman. Instead, he stood a little taller. "The poor thing."

The couple chuckled.

"Well, she's adorable," the woman said as they walked away.

Audrey wasn't sure what to say. Should she call Tyler out for allowing the couple to believe they were married, or let it go? But the warmth in her chest as Willow began devouring her bottle had her keeping quiet. And entertaining ridiculous notions whose time had long passed.

Clearing her throat, she looked at Tyler. "Why don't you grab a cart and we'll start loading it."

By the time they left the store an hour later, Audrey was pushing a shopping cart that not only held Willow, but lights, lighted garlands and extension cords, while Tyler maneuvered a flatbed cart boasting the Nativity and deer, along with an inflatable snowman that was too cute to resist. Enough to make a good starting point.

With the bed of the truck full, they decided

to skip the other store for now and head back to the ranch. While Willow slept in the back seat, silence stretched between Audrey and Tyler, though she couldn't decide if it was awkward or companionable. Strange how their lives had become so entwined. Never in a million years would she have imagined they'd be working together again. But Tyler still got her. He had a knack for understanding what she was thinking even when she couldn't put it into words.

"You're awful quiet over there." He glanced across the center console. "Everything alright?"

"Yes, I'm just contemplating what's going to go where and what else I might want to add." Her phone beeped, and she retrieved it from her back pocket to check the screen. "Oh! Looks like we've got another booking."

"That's great. At the bunkhouse?" he asked as she tapped the screen to read.

Her smile evaporated as her heart dropped into her stomach. "Oh, no."

"What is it?" He maneuvered his truck over the cattle guard at the ranch entrance.

"It's not for the bunkhouse. It's for the log cabin. But how can that be? I had it blocked." She pulled up the calendar on the Web site and studied it. Then heaved a sigh. "I only blocked out the days through the end of October. Friday is November first." At the time, she'd thought that would be plenty of time. But things had changed.

"Okay." He glanced her way, maneuvering up the winding road and into the woods. "Could Willow and I stay at the bunkhouse?"

"No, it's booked, too."

"Oh, yeah, you said that." He rounded the drive in front of the ranch house and parked.

There's an extra bedroom at the ranch house.

As quickly as the thought popped into her head, she dismissed it. No, no. She and Tyler might be managing a civil relationship, but then they'd go their separate ways. Being in the same house with him would be different. Awkward. And so not happening.

She opened her door and stepped onto the gravel surface while Tyler retrieved Willow from the back seat. The sound of a vehicle approaching had them both looking down the drive to find Aunt Dee's pickup bumping their way. Seconds later, she pulled alongside Tyler's truck.

"How'd it go?" her aunt asked when she exited her truck.

Moving to the back of Dirk's vehicle, Audrey dropped the tailgate as her aunt joined her. "We found a few things." She gestured to the boxes in the truck bed.

Dee cocked her head, eyeing the images on the sides of the boxes. "I like those. They'll look real nice."

"And we also got a ton of lights and garland." Audrey sighed.

The cowgirl glanced Tyler's way as he joined them, holding Willow's carrier, his expression every bit as conflicted as Audrey felt. "What's wrong?" Her gaze darted back to Audrey.

"I received a notification of another booking."

"That's good news. How come you're not smilin'?"

"Because it's for the log cabin." Audrey felt her shoulders fall. "I only had the dates blocked out through the end of October."

Nodding, Dee said, "Oh, I see where you're comin' from." She looked at Tyler. "Sorry to inconvenience you like that, but we'll get you and Willow fixed up, don't you worry." Her gaze fell to the infant. "Yes we will, sweetheart."

Willow cooed in response.

"We've got an extra bedroom here, so y'all can just stay with us. Yes you can, you sweet doll."

Audrey felt her eyes widen.

As if sensing her unease, Tyler said, "That's not necessary, Aunt Dee. I don't want to inconvenience you. Willow and I can spend the weekend at a hotel."

The older woman straightened, a scowl on her face. "You most certainly will not. You're the one who's being inconvenienced, not us."

"But Willow's apt to wake up at all hours of the night," he countered.

"So am I." Dee perched her hands on her hips, digging in for a fight she obviously intended to win.

Tyler looked Audrey's way, as if he was waiting for her input. Like she could overrule Aunt Dee.

With a sigh, she said, "You'll need to have most of your things out of the cabin the night before, then everything else needs to be gone by 8:00 a.m. so I can clean and prep it for guests."

"I'll help, too." Her aunt nodded. "We can take turns watchin' Willow."

Audrey lifted her chin. "I guess that's settled then. Now, let's get this stuff unloaded." As soon as that was done, she'd need to block out some more dates. Otherwise, she'd be the one contemplating a hotel.

Tyler loaded his tools into his truck the following Thursday, thankful he was back on track with the tent cabins. Saturday's beautiful weather had hung around into the workweek, allowing him to make some significant progress. He'd completed two platforms and had started on the third. Now that he'd gotten into a rhythm, things should move faster—which was probably for the best. Because while he was in no hurry to leave Legacy Ranch, he had a feeling his welcome was starting to wear thin. At least where Audrey was concerned.

And here he'd thought they might be turning a corner when she'd asked him to go shopping with her. Their conversation over lunch had been pleasant. At the store, it felt like old times when she verbally painted a picture of what she wanted, and he pointed her in the right direction. He'd always loved the way her face lit up as her plans began to take shape.

But her obvious dismay over him staying at the ranch house had been an abrupt reminder that any relationship between them was strictly business. And he'd do well to keep his distance.

The sound of tires on gravel had him glancing toward the lush, sun-drenched landscape to find Dirk's pickup approaching.

"What's up?" Tyler asked minutes later when Dirk emerged from his vehicle and started his way, his faithful sidekick, Molly, at his side.

"I just got off the phone with Mr. Bruce Hendricks."

"Oh, yeah." Tyler tugged his ball cap a little lower. Dirk had spoken with the man earlier, but then had to send Bruce some photos of the barn. "Did you get your quote?"

"A rough one. He still needs to come and inspect things so he can avoid any surprises."

"And?"

"It was reasonable. Comparable with my guy."

Tyler eyed the man who was quickly becoming a friend. "Then why do you look so concerned?"

Gazing past Tyler to his work in progress, Dirk sucked a deep breath. "Seems they had a cancellation. If everything checks out, and we're in agreement, he'd like to start a week from Monday."

Tyler felt his eyes widen. "That quick, huh? Audrey will be thrilled." He could imagine her mind shifting gears faster than a NASCAR driver.

"Probably, but it means I'll need to get the barn ready, and I've got a guy coming out next week with a skid steer to start clearing the site for Tessa's and my house."

Crossing his arms, Tyler said, "I could help you out with the barn. What all needs to be done?"

"There are some old pens that need to be removed, along with the hayloft, not to mention an old tractor. Probably should remove some of the siding, too."

Watching Molly lie down in the grass, Tyler said, "I'd be happy to do it." Only after the words tumbled out did he consider the ramifications. Namely Audrey. Helping at the barn meant putting the platforms on hold, delaying their completion. And extending his stay.

"You sure?" Dirk eyed Tyler's work in progress. "Audrey's pretty eager for you to get things done here."

"I know. However, she's already indicated this barn is an even bigger deal." Though how she'd feel about him hanging around even longer remained to be seen. "The sooner you can get going on it, the sooner it'll be finished."

Squinting against the sun, Dirk said, "When are you planning to go back to Fort Worth?"

"I'm kind of playing that by ear while I sort through my options. I don't want to wear out my welcome here, but as long as there are things to keep me busy—" He took in the pastoral setting. "It's peaceful here. Makes it easier to think." He looked at Dirk again. "Know what I mean?"

"I sure do. My late wife and I lived in Austin. After growing up in the country, city life took some getting used to."

Tyler studied the other man. "If you don't mind me asking, what happened to your wife?"

Dirk toed at the ground with his boot. "Car accident. It took Lindsey, our four-year-old daughter, Harper, and the lower part of my left leg." He hoisted his pant leg a notch, revealing a prosthetic.

"Wow. That's rough." And Tyler thought he'd gone through some tough stuff. "I'm sorry, man. Having lost my sister in a car wreck—" not to mention everyone else in his family in one form or another "—I know how earth-shattering that can be. But your wife and kid?" He rubbed the back of his neck. "I can't imagine."

"I'm not gonna lie. There were days I didn't want to go on. But God is good. He brought Tessa into my life. Suddenly, I didn't feel quite so alone."

"You both lost your spouses."

Dirk nodded. "We know how fragile love can be and have learned not to take it for granted."

Tyler thought about his and Audrey's relationship. The way he took her for granted. He'd kept her at arm's length while she dealt with the greatest struggle of her life.

Dragging a hand over his face, he said, "Tessa's a good woman."

"Yes, she is." Dirk's smile grew. "I'm blessed to have her. And I couldn't love Grayson and Bryce more if they were my own flesh and blood."

"So when's the wedding?"

"March." He hiked a brow. "Maybe Audrey will ask you to be her date."

Tyler snorted, shaking his head. "That ship has sailed, man." And it was all his fault. "I hurt her pretty badly."

Dirk cocked his head. "Was that BC?"

"BC?"

"Before Christ. Were either of you believers back then?"

"No."

Sporting a goofy grin, Dirk said, "Then don't discount it. Like the Bible says, with God, all things are possible."

Tyler might grasp that in his head, but his heart scoffed at the notion. Hoping to change the subject, he said, "Back to the barn—don't you have a crew?"

The other man looked rather chagrinned. "I'm

kind of a one-man show. I've got a couple of guys I call in when I need extra help. Which was fine when I was doing mostly smaller jobs. Since starting at Legacy Ranch, I've been getting a lot more calls for bids, which has me wondering if it's time to expand. Especially now that I'll have a family, and Tessa and I will be building our own home here at the ranch."

"So what's holding you back?"

"What else? Fear."

Tyler stroked the scruff on his chin. "Interesting. So was this BC?"

Dirk laughed. "Touché." A second later, he said, "You own your own business, right?"

"Yes, I'm part owner of a homebuilding company."

"How many partners?"

"Just two of us. We're not huge, but things have taken off." Tyler eyed Dirk. "Back to your original question, about me pushing the pause button here—" he poked a thumb over his shoulder "—perhaps you should run the idea past Audrey to see what she says. I'm more than happy to stay longer, so long as it doesn't upset her."

Dirk eyed him as though he wanted to ask him something but seemed to stop himself. "I'll do that."

"Good. Now, I'm going to call it a day because I need to get Willow's and my things out of the log cabin."

"I heard there was a little conflict."

"We worked it out. Though I don't think Audrey's too happy about me staying at the ranch house."

Dirk grinned. "She's not happy? You're going to be the only dude among three strong-willed women, two boys and an infant."

"You left out the partridge in a pear tree."

Dirk laughed. "You're a braver man than I am."

"Thankfully, I've got Aunt Dee in my corner, so maybe it won't be too bad."

At least he hoped not. So long as he didn't do anything to upset Audrey. But then, he seemed to excel at that.

Chapter Seven

First Audrey was forced to spend a weekend in the same house as Tyler, and now he was going to remain at the ranch for who knew how much longer. No wonder she hadn't been able to sleep. Her only consolation was that the timeline for the barn had been bumped up considerably. So by the time Tyler and Willow were gone, she'd have her hands full overseeing every aspect of the building's transformation from forsaken barn to show-stopping venue.

At the kitchen table early Saturday morning, she nursed her second cup of coffee. Aunt Dee had already left to tend to her to-do list, but everyone else was still asleep. Even Willow.

Dee had insisted Tyler and Willow take her room downstairs while she slept in the smaller room upstairs. Not only did her room have more space for the portable crib, it also had a private bath. And given that the only bathroom upstairs was shared by Audrey and Tessa, not to mention Tessa's two sons, it was in high demand.

The switch also provided more distance between Audrey and Tyler. Though with her room directly over the downstairs suite, she'd awakened every time Willow did. Then she lay there in the darkness, listening as Tyler quietly tended the infant's needs. Audrey might not have been able to make out what he was saying, but the sound of his deep voice had her imagining what their life might have been like had their baby lived. Would Tyler have been as attentive to their child as he was with Willow? Would he have been onboard for 3:00 a.m. feedings, allowing Audrey to get some extra sleep?

Downing the last of her coffee, she shook off the ridiculous notions and set her cup on the table. What was done was done. Why torture herself?

After starting another pot of coffee, she snuck upstairs to her room where she traded her baggy pajama bottoms and two-sizes-too-big T-shirt for jeans and a dark green pullover with three-quarter-length sleeves. Then, as she threw her hair into a messy bun, she remembered the reason Tyler was here—because the bunkhouse *and* the log cabin were booked. Just the thought had her doing a little happy dance.

Guests for both had checked in late yesterday, and all appeared to be happy with their accommodations. The couple at the bunkhouse were oohing and aahing, expressing how much their three kids were going to enjoy it. Audrey had made sure the firepit was ready to be lit, and as she was leaving, she heard them talking about the hot dogs and marshmallows they were going to roast.

Now she shoved her feet into her slip-on sneakers and made her way back downstairs. Only four months ago, Audrey and her sisters had sat at Aunt Dee's dining room table, listening as she laid out her dreams for the ranch. Her desire to create a place where people could enjoy a different lifestyle. One that moved at a leisurely pace and made people smile. And once she had the opportunity, Aunt Dee was ready to take the bull by the horns.

This weekend, those dreams were coming to life. And that called for a celebration.

So, after pouring herself another cup of coffee, Audrey set to work on breakfast—her superfluffy pancakes and lots of bacon.

As the aroma of their favorite breakfast meat permeated the kitchen, a bed head–sporting Tyler wandered into the room with Willow.

Audrey couldn't help chuckling. "I see some things never change."

Pausing beside the coffeepot, he sent her a curious look. "What?"

"The scent of bacon could always pull you out of the deepest sleep."

He grabbed a mug. "Willow must've inherited it from me, because she's the one who woke me up." After filling his cup, he sat down at the table. "I hope her fussing didn't keep you awake last night."

Audrey dropped a scoop of pancake batter onto the griddle. "Nah, I barely heard her." Her uncle, on the other hand... She caught a glimpse of him as he nursed his coffee, and it reminded her of lazy Sunday mornings at their house in Fort Worth. Now they spent Sunday mornings at church. Would things have been different if they had been believers back then?

Shaking her head, she returned her attention to the food. No point in entertaining what-ifs.

"Somethin' smells good." Grayson entered the room and joined her at the stove. "Mmm, pancakes *and* bacon." He licked his lips.

"Yes, sir. We're celebrating that the cabin and the bunkhouse both have guests. Why don't you go tell your mom and your brother?"

"Okay."

Audrey moved the pancakes to a plate and was adding more batter to the griddle when Aunt Dee entered from the carriage porch.

"Mmm...smells good in here!" she hollered from the laundry room.

"I hope you're hungry, because breakfast is almost ready."

Her own stomach growling, Audrey settled two steaming platters of food atop the dining room table a short time later.

With Willow in one arm, Tyler pulled out a chair. "This looks delicious."

"Audrey's pancakes are hard to beat." Aunt Dee took her seat at the head of the table.

Across from Audrey, Tyler caught her eye. "I remember."

Thoughts of those lazy mornings had Audrey's cheeks heating.

Once Tessa and her boys were settled, Aunt Dee said grace and silence ensued as everyone dug in. Until Audrey's phone rang.

Glancing at the screen, she recognized the number as one of their guests.

"Hello, this is Audrey."

"Audrey, this is Camy Stewart." The mom of the crew at the bunkhouse. "We have a bit of a problem."

Laying her fork atop her plate, Audrey's heart all but stopped.

"The toilet is overflowing," Camy continued. "My husband turned off the water, but I think it might be clogged or something."

"Don't worry. I'll be there just as quick as I can." All eyes were on Audrey as she ended the call and pushed out her chair. "The toilet's overflowing at the bunkhouse. I need to go check it out."

"That's brand-new plumbin'." Her aunt frowned. "I wonder what it could be."

"I don't know," said Audrey, "but I need to go find out."

"I'll go with you." Tyler was on his feet now, Willow still cradled in his arm.

"We can't take Willow," said Audrey.

"I'll watch her." Tessa stood and rounded the table to Tyler. "Come here, sweet girl."

"Thanks, sis."

While Tyler changed clothes, Audrey located a plunger, clueless as to what else she might need.

As they headed outside into the crisp morning air minutes later, Tyler said, "We may as well take the truck since my toolbox is in there."

"Good idea. Thanks." She threw herself into the passenger seat while Tyler fired up the engine. "How could this happen? Everything is brand-new." She huffed. "Nothing like making a bad first impression. This could ruin everything we've worked toward."

"Don't be so hard on yourself." Tyler gripped the steering wheel with both hands as they started down the drive. "Like you said, everything is new. So either something malfunctioned or there's a clog somewhere."

"Where, though?" She glanced across the console. "I mean, it's hardly been used."

"Alright, the first thing you need to do is calm down. Freaking out is not going to help the situation. So take a deep breath and settle down.

Worst-case scenario, you refund their money and offer them a discount on their next booking."

Why hadn't she thought of that?

"And it wouldn't hurt to bring God into the equation," he added, "so bow your head."

"What?"

"You heard me." His smile had her complying. "Lord God, we thank You for the guests You brought to Legacy Ranch this weekend. I'd hate for this incident to ruin their time here or reflect badly on Audrey. So we commit this situation into Your hands, trusting that You will work all things together for good as Your word says. Give us wisdom to find the problem and, if possible, make it a quick fix. We pray this in Jesus's name, amen."

Audrey couldn't decide if she was shocked or humbled. Tyler had prayed. That certainly hadn't been her first instinct. Instead, she'd freaked. "Thank you, Tyler. I needed to hear that."

Soon they pulled up to the wooden structure that had once served as a home for the ranch's many cowboys and hired hands, though it had sat empty for as long as Audrey could remember, not much more than a dilapidated shack. But Aunt Dee saw promise in it, and with Dirk's help, the structure was now a quaint getaway for families, complete with a sleeping loft for kids. Or anyone young at heart.

Stepping out of the truck, Audrey noticed nothing but ashes in the firepit, and that made her smile.

Tyler grabbed his toolbox and the plunger before joining her. "Ready?"

"Yep."

Leaves rustled in the trees as they started toward the inviting building. Its once-whitewashed cottonwood siding now boasted a medium brownish-gray hue that paired well with the new green metal roof and blended beautifully into its surroundings.

The door opened then, and three little ones—two boys and a girl—ranging from about four to eight years of age stepped onto the porch, followed by their parents.

"We are *so* sorry to bother you." Camy looked as though she felt just as bad, if not worse, than Audrey did.

"Not a problem." Audrey continued toward them.

"I turned the water off as soon as I saw what was happening," said Graham, Camy's husband.

"And I sopped up the water with towels." Camy winced. "So we might need some more."

"We have plenty at the ranch house, don't you worry." Audrey couldn't believe how calm she sounded. "I'm going to let Tyler here—" she poked a thumb over her shoulder "—have a look at things."

"You'll have to excuse the mess in the kitchen,"

Camy said. "We were having breakfast when we saw the water."

Audrey followed Tyler into the quaint structure, which looked nothing like its former self and smelled of pancake syrup. While he continued inside the small bathroom with a shower, vanity and commode, she watched from the doorway as he set his toolbox on the vinyl plank floor. Then he removed the lid on the tank and studied it for a minute.

"What are you looking for?" she asked.

"Anything out of the ordinary. It's a brand-new commode, so things should be fine, but you never know."

After replacing the lid, he lifted the seat. "Hand me that plunger, please." Then, before taking hold, he stooped. Dropped to his knees.

"What is it?"

"I'm not sure." He opened his toolbox and retrieved a pair of long-handled pliers. Then he rolled up his sleeves before plunging the pliers into the water. Thankfully, the water was clear, and the toilet was new. Though she still cringed.

"There's something stuck right there." He poked around the drain, his face contorting as he tried to maneuver the pliers. "This is going to take two hands." Seconds later, he said, "Got it." Then he held up what looked like a drowned stuffed animal as the remaining water disappeared down the drain. "That was easy." He pushed to his feet. "Hand me a towel."

She did, though instead of wiping his hands, he held the waterlogged critter over the towel and stepped past her.

"Anyone recognize this?"

"Eww... Fluffy is all yucky," the little girl cried.

Meanwhile, her brothers snickered.

"Boys...?" Graham glared at his sons.

After depositing the waterlogged critter in the trash, Tyler returned to the bathroom to turn the water back on and make sure the commode was working properly, while Audrey assured Camy she would be back shortly with a fresh set of towels. Then she recommended a couple of shops in Brenham where they might be able to find a replacement for the drowned toy.

Back inside the truck, Audrey breathed a sigh of relief.

"Disaster averted." Tyler smiled.

"Thanks to you." Eyeing him across the cab, she found herself wondering if she'd been judging him too harshly. And what she would've done if he hadn't been with her.

Tyler retrieved his lunch cooler from his truck shortly after noon the following Wednesday, then aimed for the pretty little pond that sat beyond the old wooden barn. It made the perfect setting for a wedding or just about any other event. Peaceful. Picturesque.

What a beautiful November day. Not a cloud in the sky. Temperatures hovering around seventy degrees. Too nice to be cooped up inside. Even if inside was a bit of a misnomer given all the barn's missing boards.

While Dirk spent today at his future homesite, Tyler was dismantling some old pens in the barn, taking care to salvage the wood, including some ancient bois d'arc posts. Those things could last forever.

After their meeting with Bruce Hendricks on Monday, Aunt Dee and Dirk had given the go-ahead to get things started, which had Audrey almost bouncing out of her cute little sneakers. Her smile was huge. It had Tyler recalling a time when he'd been able to make her smile like that.

Approaching the shimmering water, he noticed a crude bench perched beneath an oak tree. After determining it was sturdy, he sat down and pulled out the chicken-fried steak sandwich leftover from last night's supper that had been calling his name all morning.

He took a hearty bite, the mayo complementing the ultimate comfort food as he stared out over the pond. Too bad he didn't have a fishing pole.

When his phone interrupted his reverie, he eyed the screen before tapping the speaker icon. "Hey, Reid."

"Well, don't you sound chipper."

"Because I'm in paradise." He set his sandwich aside and opened his camera app. "Get a load of this." Then he snapped a shot of the pond and sent it to his partner before taking another bite of his sandwich.

"Nice! Is that at the ranch?"

Tyler swallowed. "Yep. It sits behind that old barn I told you about."

"The one they want to turn into a venue?" Since they talked a few times each week, Tyler had kept his partner up-to-date on all the goings-on around the ranch.

"That's the one. It's so peaceful, I decided to eat my lunch out here."

"Not quite what you expected when you landed there almost a month ago, is it?"

Tyler snorted, shaking his head. "Not at all. It's kinda wild. Yet despite staying busy, I've found more clarity about Willow's and my future."

"Manual labor combined with a good support system will do that for you. Plus you and Willow are better acquainted. You're settling into the new role God's called you to."

Though Reid couldn't see him, Tyler nodded as he chewed another bite.

"How are things with you and Audrey?"

Tyler swallowed. "Depends on the day. She's hot and cold. Most of the time, she tolerates me, at best. I try not to let it get to me, and instead, help her any way I can."

"From the sound of it, there's no shortage of things to keep you busy."

"Not at all. I don't mind, though. I actually enjoy it. And it eases my conscience. I hurt Audrey pretty bad, so it feels good to see her smile." Like she had after he solved the problem at the bunkhouse Saturday. He felt the corners of his mouth lift. He'd plunge his bare hands into even the nastiest of toilets if it made her happy.

"Have you considered apologizing and asking her to forgive you?" Reid asked. "After all, you're not the same man who allowed her to walk out of his life. You're a new creation in Christ."

A crow cawed in the distance as Tyler contemplated his friend's suggestion. "What if she won't forgive me?"

"Then you carry on, knowing you were sincere. God will honor that."

Tyler sighed. "I'll have to pray on that one, man." And continue doing whatever he could to try to earn his way back into her good graces.

After saying goodbye to Reid, Tyler finished his lunch, including two of the chocolate chip cookies Audrey had made yesterday. Man, he'd eaten better since coming to Legacy Ranch than he had in years. Thankfully, the work he'd been doing had kept him moving, otherwise he'd be needing some larger pants.

Staring out over the glorious setting, he prayed. "God, I still can't believe I'm here. That I'm *still* here in this beautiful place. You've orchestrated events that have brought Audrey and me back together. To bring healing and, perhaps, closure. I guess closure is what had me setting out for Houston a month ago. Though I'm still seeking it. Is Reid right? Should I ask Audrey to forgive me?" Elbows on his knees, hands clasped, he shook his head. "Your word says that 'if any man be in Christ, he is a new creature.' I know that You've transformed my life, but can others see that? Can Audrey see it?"

That last question stuck with him as he returned to the barn. He pulled up some Crowder on his phone and turned up the volume before retrieving the crowbar and hammer and setting to work again. He sure wished he could be here to see this place transformed. Dirk had clued him in on the plans to expand the barn's original footprint, adding wings onto the sides that would provide space for a kitchen and bathrooms, as well as dressing rooms and storage. Not to mention a wall of windows that would overlook that beautiful pond.

Audrey was correct in her assertion that the ranch's proximity to Houston and Austin would make this a desirable location for many an event. And with her running the show, he had no doubt it would be a huge success.

Movement outside the open door had him looking that way as Audrey's vehicle came to a stop. She emerged from the front seat before opening the back door, no doubt retrieving Willow.

He turned off his music and moved toward the door as Audrey started in his direction. The way her hair bounced around her shoulders, Willow in her arms, nearly took his breath away. What a picture the two of them made. One that hit him in the gut as he became fully aware of all he'd lost. The family he'd always longed for. A loving wife, kids... Yet he'd let that dream slip through his fingers because he'd been too proud, too insecure, too selfish to allow himself to be vulnerable.

God had given him the desires of his heart, and Tyler had been too foolish to recognize it for the gift that it was.

The realization was almost too much to bear. What he wouldn't give for a do-over.

God, forgive me. And, if possible, let Audrey forgive me.

"How's it going?" Wearing a gray T-shirt over black joggers and sneakers, she sent him a smile that went straight to his heart. And had him feeling like the world's biggest loser for what he'd done to her. Or *not* done. What kind of man lets his wife grieve alone?

"Not too bad." He palmed Willow's downy

head when Audrey stopped in front of him. "What brings you two out here?"

"It's such a beautiful day, I thought Little Miss here might enjoy some fresh air." She pulled one corner of her bottom lip between her teeth. "And I may have been just a tad bit curious as to what's happening here." She peered past him. "Looks like you're making progress."

"Slowly, but yes."

She eyed the pile of discarded wood. "I hope you're planning to keep all of that."

"Don't worry. Dirk already told me." Even if he hadn't, Tyler knew better.

"Good. These pieces are part of the ranch's history, so I'd like to utilize as much as possible in the finished product. Even if it's only for decorative purposes."

"Like you did at our house." Anything he removed, Audrey had scrutinized and cataloged in case she found some way to use it. She was good at thinking outside the box.

Her gaze found his. "Exactly."

Suddenly flustered, he said, "Check out these old pens over here." He started that way, his heart thudding as he ducked under a rail. As he started to rise, his head collided with something, jolting his entire body while flashes of light blurred his vision. He heard Audrey's gasp. Then he stumbled, landing on his rear end.

"Tyler, are you okay?"

He moved a hand to the back of his head, trying to regain his wits. "What happened?"

Kneeling near him with Willow in her arms, Audrey said, "You stood too soon and hit your head on the rail."

"Yeah, I don't recommend that."

"No kidding." She stood. "Stay right there. I'm going to get Willow's carrier out of the car, so I can put her in it while I help you up."

"That's alright." He groped for something to help him stand. "I'll be fine."

"No, you will *not*. I mean it, Tyler. You stay put until I can help you or, so help me, I will hurt you myself."

Chapter Eight

Just when Tyler thought things were getting better with Audrey, he had to go and embarrass himself. Now, as he rested on the sofa at the log cabin later that afternoon, per Aunt Dee and Audrey's orders, he felt like a chump.

While Audrey had feared he might have a concussion after whacking his head on one of the rails in the barn, Aunt Dee suggested that, since he hadn't lost consciousness, he was probably alright. Then she insisted he rest for the remainder of the day, while Audrey offered to stay with him to make sure he behaved. What was he, twelve?

Now Willow slept in her crib, while the sizzle of meat in the kitchen had been replaced with the aroma of something tangy, making his stomach growl. So as the light grew dim outside, he stood and crossed a handful of feet to the kitchen.

Peering around the corner, he found Audrey standing at the stove, stirring whatever was in the pot with one hand while empty tomato sauce cans sat on the counter beside her. "Whatcha cooking?"

She started. Frowning at him, she said, "You're supposed to be on the couch."

"You shouldn't tempt me to get up." He rubbed his midsection. "My stomach's making all kinds of noise."

Retrieving a spice jar from the counter, she said, "This chili will need to simmer for a while, so you go sit back down and I'll be there shortly."

"Promise?"

Snorting, she shook her head. "You're worse than my nephews." She glanced his way. "Yes, I promise. Now, scoot."

He complied. And as he waited, he recalled his lunchtime conversation with Reid.

Have you considered apologizing and asking her to forgive you?

With his pride already in a heap, Tyler was able to recognize that it was more than just fear that had kept him from doing those things. And while he didn't believe in kicking someone when they were down, he'd already been humbled today. Might as well hang out there a while.

A few minutes passed before Audrey joined him. "How's your head feeling?"

"It only hurts if I push on the point of contact."

"No headache?"

He shook his head. "Nope."

The ridged set of her shoulders seemed to relax. "That's good."

"Is the chili simmering now?"

"Yes." She wandered around the back of the couch to check on Willow.

"In that case, would you mind sitting down? I have something I need to talk to you about." He watched as her shoulders stiffened.

Then, with an almost imperceptible nod, she rounded the couch to sit in the upholstered chair a few feet away from him, beside the stone fireplace. "What do you want to talk about?" She smoothed her hands over her jogger-covered thighs.

Staring at his clasped hands, he said, "I want to apologize for not being there for you like I should have after the miscarriage. I'd gotten so adept at hiding my own pain that I ignored yours." He looked at her now. "That was selfish and immature of me. I should've been there to walk with you through the fire, no matter how uncomfortable it made me. Because that's what marriage is all about, right?"

Eyes wide, she nodded.

"I'm sorry I wasn't the husband I should've been. The husband you deserved." He dragged his fingers through his hair. "Looking back, I never should've asked you to marry me."

Her body went rigid. "Are you saying you regret marrying me?"

He shook his head. "Only because you deserved better. I was messed up. There's so much I never told you about my life because I was afraid you'd leave me." He snorted. "How ironic that my silence had you leaving anyway."

Her gaze narrowed. "Tyler, were you doing drugs or something?"

"What? No." He shook his head. "It was nothing like that." He heaved a sigh, knowing that if he didn't come clean now, he never would. "My whole life—up until I met Jesus—was a charade."

"What does that mean?" There was an edge to her voice.

He forced himself to look at her. "I only let people see what I wanted them to see. Including you."

"Why would you do that?"

He couldn't help noticing the way her fingers dug into the padded arms on her chair. "What my dad did—leaving us—really messed me over. I thought it was my fault. That I'd done something wrong. So from then on, I buried my feelings and put on a false bravado that served me well. I got good grades. I was personable. People liked me. Yet one by one, the people who mattered most left me. My mom. My sister."

"Me." Audrey watched him.

The day she walked out, everything he'd felt when his father left had come rushing back like a tidal wave, threatening to take him under. But she didn't need to know that.

"Only because I'd abandoned you first." He cleared his throat. "Audrey, you were the best thing that ever happened to me. And I failed you miserably. You didn't deserve that." While she stared at her clasped hands, he leaned forward, resting his forearms on his thighs. "When I started going to church, I finally realized that I wasn't responsible for my parents' mistakes. Just my own. And what I did to you—deserting you after the miscarriage—was wrong. I used to think being vulnerable was a sign of weakness, so I selfishly kept my feelings to myself, leaving you to grieve alone." He captured her gaze, needing her to know he was sincere. "You deserved better, Audrey. Saying I'm sorry seems so lame, but I truly am sorry. And I pray that—one day—you might be able to forgive me."

"I forgive you." Her words came out so quickly, they had him doing a double take.

"Y-you do?" Only then did he notice the tears spilling onto her pretty cheeks.

She nodded, still not making eye contact. "That morning—before I knew I'd lost our baby—when I woke up, I didn't feel right. As if something was off." Her voice cracked. "But I ignored it because I had a big closing that day. So I got ready and pressed on as usual."

When her sob escaped, he bolted from the sofa. Kneeling beside her, he reached for her.

Holding his hand in a death grip, she continued. "When I got home that night, I was cramping. I—I started spotting." She gasped for air. "Our baby was gone. And it was my fault."

Unable to stop himself, Tyler wrapped his arms around a sobbing Audrey and held her as they grieved together. The way they should have all those years ago.

He smoothed a hand over her back, his fingers tangling in her soft hair while tears streamed down his own cheeks. He couldn't believe it. He was crying with Audrey. Him, the kid who'd always refused to cry or show any emotion.

How did the verse go? *Weeping may endure for a night, but joy cometh in the morning.* Audrey deserved joy. *God, please, bring joy into Audrey's life. Exceedingly abundant joy!*

When she pulled away, she stared at him with puffy eyes. "Can you forgive me?"

He took her face in his calloused hands, brushing away her tears with his thumbs. "There is nothing to forgive, Audrey. It wasn't your fault. You got that?"

Her questioning gaze searched his before she finally nodded.

Willow began to fuss.

"I'll get her." He pushed to his feet, needing to put some distance between him and Audrey.

Rounding the sofa, he knew the precise moment Willow spotted him, because she smiled.

Suddenly, a Christmas song infiltrated his brain. Something about a baby changing everything. And as he looked down at the precious gift his sister had left him, still pondering all he and Audrey had just shared, the way they'd bared their souls, he couldn't agree more.

A weary Audrey unloaded the dishwasher in the ranch house kitchen just before seven thirty the following morning, the aroma of coffee filling the space as a second pot brewed. Tessa and the boys had already left for school while Aunt Dee was out and about the ranch, doing whatever it was she did first thing every morning.

Audrey hadn't felt this drained since she returned to Houston after leaving Fort Worth, Tyler and the life they'd built together. But last evening, witnessing an uncharacteristically vulnerable Tyler had nearly done her in, resurrecting her own failures and mistakes.

There is nothing to forgive.

The sincerity in his light brown eyes as he'd said those words had loosened whatever it was that had held her captive to a shame that ran so deep that she'd never told anyone about her pregnancy. Not even the people she loved most.

So she'd hung around the cabin under the guise of caring for Willow and monitoring Tyler until she knew Aunt Dee and Tessa would be in bed. Then she'd quietly returned to the ranch house and made her way upstairs to her room where she'd lain in her bed, staring into the darkness for hours, replaying those awful months between the miscarriage and her departure.

She'd become a shell of herself during that time. The things that had once brought her joy—her job, working on the house—no longer held any appeal. She'd lost her child and she'd been certain she was losing Tyler, too. That he despised her, blaming her for the miscarriage.

In other words, she'd made it all about her. Pulling away from him before he could do the same to her. Because she was certain he would. And he had. Though not for the reasons she'd imagined.

Heaving a sigh, she grabbed a handful of silverware before opening a nearby drawer and sorting the utensils into their proper sections. It seemed she and Tyler were their own worst enemies. Launching preemptive strikes when the only attacks were coming from within.

How different things might have been if they'd just talked to each other. Opened up about what they were feeling, instead of retreating into themselves.

Sighing, she closed the drawer with her hip as the door from the carriage porch opened in the laundry room behind her. Turning that way, she found Nash trotting toward her, so she stooped to greet the aging Australian shepherd with a rub and pat.

"Hey there, stranger."

Audrey straightened to see Aunt Dee toeing out of her boots as the coffeepot gave a final gurgle and sigh before falling silent.

"What time did you get in last night?"

"Around ten." Then, before her aunt could ask any more questions, Audrey added, "I wanted to make sure Willow was settled in before leaving Tyler alone."

Dee came toward her in sock feet, well-worn jeans and a chambray work shirt, a sudden crease in her brow. "He doin' alright?"

"Yes. I just wanted him to rest as much as possible." *And make sure you'd be in bed so you wouldn't notice I'd been crying.*

The older woman retrieved her coffee mug from the windowsill behind the sink. "You're lookin' kinda down in the dumps this mornin'." Creases appeared in the corners of her blue eyes as she took hold of the coffeepot. "Did somethin' happen between you and Tyler?"

Audrey drew in a long breath, watching the steam rise as her aunt poured. Something had definitely happened. Though not in the way her aunt might think. Instead, their confessions had torn down the walls they'd erected, leaving them exposed and vulnerable. Something neither of them was particularly fond of, as evidenced by yesterday's events.

"You want some?" Aunt Dee gestured with the pot she still held.

"Yes, please." Audrey motioned to her cup. This was it. The time had come for her to tell her family the truth behind her divorce. And who better to start with than the one person who'd always been there for her, through good and bad, loving her no matter what. And she'd better do it before Tyler arrived with Willow at eight.

Grabbing her freshly filled mug, she eyed her aunt, forcing a smile she didn't necessarily feel. "Let's sit down at the table."

"Alright." Her aunt eyed her curiously as she started toward the round wooden table and pulled out one of the four captain's chairs. "I get the feelin' I'm not gonna like whatever it is you're 'bout to tell me."

Audrey grabbed hold of the next chair and eased into the seat. "It has to do with Tyler's and my divorce, and what really happened."

Dee's eyebrows lifted. "Did he cheat on you?"

Shaking her head, Audrey said, "No, he did not."

One brow quirked higher. "Did you cheat on him?"

Audrey shook her head. "Nobody cheated."

"Well, that's a relief." Aunt Dee pressed a hand

to her chest as she dropped into her seat. "In that case, you can go on."

"Thank you." Audrey wound her cold fingers around her mug, savoring the warmth as she pondered where to start. Not that she hadn't been contemplating her speech all night. Yet no matter her approach, every opening sounded terrible.

She took a deep breath. "Several months before I left Tyler, we learned that I was pregnant." Ignoring her aunt's gasp, Audrey forged ahead. "I was so eager to share the news with you, Daddy and my sisters, but I wanted to wait until I was through my first trimester." The air went out of her sails then. Her shoulders fell. "Except that day never came. I miscarried at nine weeks."

"Oh, darlin'." Aunt Dee reached for Audrey's hand. "Why didn't you tell us?"

"Because I felt like a failure. And that—" a tear spilled onto her cheek, but she quickly swiped it away "—it was my fault." She told her about that horrible day and how things had played out. The dreadful confirmation from her obstetrician the next day. "As I grieved—and boy, did I grieve—I could feel Tyler pulling away. He grew increasingly distant. And that made me angry."

"How come?" Her aunt's brow furrowed.

Audrey shrugged, suddenly feeling foolish. "Though I never told him I was cramping, I just knew he blamed me and had emotionally abandoned me because I lost our baby." She stared into her still-full cup. "When—in reality—retreating into myself had him dealing with his own abandonment issues from his childhood. Things he never shared with me until yesterday." She briefly filled her aunt in on all that had transpired at the cabin. How she and Tyler had each owned up to their culpability.

Shaking her head, Aunt Dee kept hold of Audrey's hand. "I'm sorry you felt you needed to go through all of that alone. We're your family, Audrey. We'd've loved you no matter what and walked through the fire with you."

"But I was the rebel." Audrey shrugged. "The one who did things my way. Moving to North Texas, eloping. I was proud that I'd made a name for myself in real estate, without riding Daddy's coattails. I was living the dream. And a baby was a part of that dream."

"Now I understand why you were so up in arms over Tyler stayin' here." Aunt Dee sighed, taking hold of her hand. "Audrey, the only person who ever lived a perfect life was Jesus. The rest of us are full of flaws. So it's useless to pretend otherwise."

"I know that now."

Dee cocked her head. "Does this mean you and Tyler are going to reconcile?"

Audrey snorted, shaking her head. "No. Too much water under the bridge."

"Not according to the Bible. It says that 'if any

man be in Christ, he is a new creature: old things are passed away; behold all things are become new.'" Aunt Dee's blue gaze remained riveted to Audrey's. "Neither you nor Tyler are the same people you were back then." She cocked her head. "Somethin' I suspect you're already discoverin' for yourself."

A knock at the front door had her pushing her chair back as trepidation knotted her stomach. "That would be Tyler and Willow."

"Want me to get it?" Her aunt stood.

"No. I'll be fine."

She continued into the center hall and toward the door. Then, with a bolstering breath, she pasted on a smile and swung open the door to find Tyler wearing a lopsided smile, his hair still damp, holding Willow in one arm, the diaper bag slung over the other shoulder, and looking every bit as uneasy as she felt. And for some strange reason, that made her smile.

Chapter Nine

By late Thursday, things at the barn had been mostly squared away, save for hauling out the old tractor, allowing Tyler to get back to work on the platforms for the tent cabins Friday morning. The third was still in the works, then there'd be one more to go. Not that he was all that eager to leave Legacy Ranch. Actually, he wouldn't mind hanging around to help finish out the interiors and see the completed product.

That would have to be Audrey's call, though. Then again, she had said she'd like to have at least one of the tent cabins completed in time for Christmas Under the Stars. And with Dirk being tied up with the goings-on at the barn, not to mention the house he and Tessa would soon be building, Audrey might need Tyler's services after all.

Amid the cool morning air, he hoisted his folding worktable from the bed of his truck. Seemed fall had finally arrived, bringing with it crisp mornings, pleasant afternoons and the kind of evenings that had one longing to sit around a campfire. Maybe he could make use of the firepit in the backyard at the cabin this weekend.

Once he unloaded his tools—power and otherwise—he surveyed the platform he'd abandoned a week ago to work on the barn. After refreshing his memory, he set to work, and it didn't take him long to get back into a groove. How he loved the scent of fresh-cut lumber.

When he paused for a coffee break, he found his thoughts drifting to Audrey. Something he couldn't afford while working with power tools, though he supposed she was never far from his mind. Especially after what had happened Wednesday.

Moving to the top of the rise, he stared out over the pasture dotted with white Charolais, still finding it hard to believe that he'd cried like a baby in front of Audrey. That they'd cried together. Yet he wasn't ashamed—at least not about the crying. Though the knowledge that he hadn't been there for Audrey and learning that she'd thought he blamed her for what had happened to the life they'd created nearly wrecked him. How could he have been so callous? To his wife, no less. The woman he'd promised to love, honor and cherish. What he'd done was purely selfish.

Yet she forgave him.

He took another swig from the insulated tumbler. If he left Legacy Ranch today with nothing more than her forgiveness, he would consider himself blessed. Yet his heart desired so much more. Things he wasn't worthy of. Like a second chance with Audrey.

Shaking off the notion, he returned the now-empty container to the tailgate and went back to work for who knew how long, until he glimpsed a white vehicle approaching, making his pulse race. Recalling what had happened the last time she'd paid him a surprise visit, he eyed his surroundings for any possible dangers. The last thing he wanted was to embarrass himself again.

He moved to meet Audrey as she got out of her SUV. "To what do I owe this unexpected surprise?"

"Willow and I decided to bring you some lunch." She pushed her door closed.

"I already have a lunch."

"A sandwich?"

"Ham and pepper jack."

"Hmm." She touched her index finger to her chin. "Not a bad combination. But nowhere near as delicious as my chicken tortilla soup with lots of chicken, beans and corn."

"Wait." He held up a hand. "*Your* chicken tortilla soup? The one I used to beg you to make all the time?"

Sending him a satisfied smile, she said, "That's the one." Then she moved to the back door, opened it and leaned inside to retrieve Willow's carrier. She passed it to him. "You hold her while I get the food."

"My truck's in the shade. I'll clear off the back and we can tailgate."

"Good idea. I brought a blanket, too." Audrey seemed to be in an exceptional mood, though he wasn't about to ask why. He was just glad to have her there.

"Come on, Willow." After clearing off the tailgate, he set the carrier holding his niece in the truck bed before making space for the food, as well as him and Audrey. His heart thudded with anticipation, though he knew he shouldn't read too much into the gesture. But hey, he was about to enjoy his favorite soup with two of his favorite people. That made for one outstanding day.

A whisper of a breeze rustled the leaves as Audrey joined them, a picnic basket hanging from her arm. After setting the basket on the bed, she lifted the lid and pulled out bowls and spoons before reaching for a large thermos. She unscrewed the lid, releasing the tantalizing aromas of chicken, garlic, chili powder and cumin.

His stomach growled, causing her to look his way. "Hungry?"

"Do you know how long it's been since I've had this soup?" Foolish question. Of course she knew he hadn't had it since their divorce. He cleared his throat. "My all-time favorite soup, I might add."

That earned him a smile.

He watched as she poured two bowls of the steaming broth laden with meat and vegetables. "I thought you might be doing some last-minute things at the bunkhouse today." She'd told him the place was booked for the next two weekends, as well as part of Thanksgiving week.

"Save for dropping off some extra towels and goodies for s'mores, it's ready to go." She handed him a steaming bowl of soup. "Careful, it's hot."

He waited until she perched alongside him on the tailgate with her own bowl and a bag of tortilla chips before grabbing his first spoonful. Then he blew on it and tested it before taking his first bite.

"Mmm." He closed his eyes, savoring the hint of lime that highlighted the other flavors. Swallowing, he pointed to the bowl with his now-empty spoon. "I can't tell you how much I've missed this." And her. "Nobody makes tortilla soup like you, Audrey."

Pink bloomed on her cheeks, and she looked almost bashful. "Thank you." Using her spoon, she poked at the black beans, corn and chicken in her own bowl. "With the cooler weather, I thought it would be appropriate."

He swallowed another bite, shaking his head. "No, this is appropriate no matter what the weather."

Setting her bowl aside, she tore open the bag of

chips and dumped some into another bowl then placed it between them.

He grabbed a couple, eyeing a now-sleeping Willow behind them.

While he continued to eat, Audrey had yet to take a bite. Then again, it was kind of hot.

Poking at her soup again—only with a chip this time—she said, "I'm starting to feel bad about taking up so much of your time. After all, your goal was to determine the logistics of your life moving forward with Willow. Yet Dirk and I have monopolized your time with work."

"You're not monopolizing anything. Actually, you've provided me with a nice change of pace. Besides, you know I like to keep busy." He looked around. "And being surrounded by all this beauty is relaxing, not chaotic like the city." Then he thought about all the time Audrey was having to spend caring for Willow while he worked. "The flip side of that coin, though, is it means you have Willow more often than not. Taking away time you could be devoting to all the projects here at the ranch."

Audrey nibbled on a chip. "I don't mind. She's a good baby. And since she's not mobile yet, it's not like I have to chase her around. Besides, it's good practice for me."

His gaze instinctively darted to her stomach before returning to her face. Surely Audrey wasn't pregnant. Not only wasn't she married, she hadn't even indicated she had a boyfriend. Besides, that scenario didn't jive with her faith. "Practice?"

"It's not what you're thinking." She sent him a lopsided grin. "I'm not pregnant. However, I am hoping to adopt a baby at some point in the not-so-distant future."

He stared unseeing into his bowl, his appetite gone. Why hadn't he realized all those years ago how strongly she felt about motherhood? No wonder her grief over the miscarriage ran so deep. Yet instead of staying by her side, offering comfort and sharing in her sorrow, he'd ignored her. She didn't deserve that. No, she deserved a husband who loved her beyond measure. And that man would never be him. He'd blown his chance.

"Tha-that's great, Audrey. You're going to be a wonderful mother." He looked at her now. "Any child would be blessed to have you."

A blush crept into her cheeks. "Thank you. It's something I'm looking forward to, though it'll be a little ways down the road. Come January, I expect I'll be busier than ever once things get going on the barn." She finally took her first bite.

"I have no doubt the venue is going to be great. I mean, just look at what you did with our place. You turned a ramshackle old house into the envy of the neighborhood."

She smiled. "Only because I had the best handyman in town. I might have had the ideas, but you executed them." She lifted a shoulder. "You made me look good."

From where he sat, he thought she looked pretty good in her own right. "We made a good team."

"Too bad we didn't communicate as well off the field." Her gaze met his. "In the things that really mattered."

"That was BC. We were different people then."

A breeze tossed her hair as she eyed him curiously. "BC?"

He chuckled. "Before Christ came into our lives." He shrugged. "I picked that up from Dirk."

"I'm glad you found Jesus, Tyler."

"Me, too. And right back atcha." He stared at his soup, poking the chunks of meat and vegetables with his spoon as he mustered some courage. "I have a request."

"What's that?"

He looked at her. "Could I *not* be your ex-husband anymore, and just be your friend?" He shrugged. "I mean, like the Bible says, 'if any man be in Christ, he is a new creature: old things are passed away; behold all things are become new.'"

Her gaze fell away. Focusing on the pasture, she sucked in a long breath.

His gut tightened. He was asking too much too soon. "I'm sorry. I shouldn't—"

She twisted to face him. "Yes, I think I'd like that very much."

"You would? I mean, okay. Good."

The sun was well on its way toward the western horizon when Audrey crossed the cattle guard at Legacy Ranch late Saturday afternoon. She'd been gone since midmorning, traveling to Brenham first, then to West Houston in search of furnishings for the tent cabins. Thanks to years of staging homes, she had an eye for detail, so pulling together the right look was second nature. Doing so at the right price presented a greater challenge, but she was up to the task.

Today, she'd come across some simple iron daybeds at one of the furniture stores in Brenham, so she ordered those, along with mattresses. In Houston, she'd found the perfect light fixtures. Made of black metal, the rectangular chandeliers had the combination rustic/industrial vibe she'd wanted. The fact that they were on sale had her happy dancing.

Then she found some great side table lamps that were so deeply discounted she snatched up all eight that remained on the shelf. Throw in some clearance towels and pillows and, needless to say, her vehicle was filled to the brim. She ought to consider bringing a truck next time.

Thoughts of a truck had her mind drifting back to yesterday and her tailgate lunch with Tyler. Her *friend* Tyler. She couldn't help chuckling. There was a time when she would've considered Tyler her best friend. Prior to her miscarriage, she'd always been open and honest with him about everything. Yet he hadn't trusted her enough to return the favor.

She got it, though, now that she had a better understanding. Aside from her mother's death, Audrey had led a rather idyllic life. She'd always been able to count on her family to be there for her, even when she was determined to do things her way. They were why she'd returned to Houston after leaving Tyler. They gave her a safe place to land and loved her despite her mistakes.

But Tyler hadn't been so blessed. She could only imagine how heartbreaking it must've been to watch his own father turn his back on him, his mother and Carrie. Audrey ached for the little boy who'd been forced to grow up too soon. Even more so now that she, too, knew the sting of abandonment.

How differently might things have turned out if she and Tyler had grieved together instead of pulling away from each other? Sadly, she'd never know. But thankfully, they'd found a measure of closure. Not to mention better insight into one another. Enough to say they were friends.

The vehicle bumped over another cattle guard before she reached the house. Then she realized she had another problem. Where was she going to store the items she'd bought? Maybe in the spare bedroom for the time being.

After turning off the engine, she retrieved as many bags as she could carry from the passenger seat and exited her vehicle. The evening air was crisp and still, the sky cloudless. What a great night to be outdoors.

She trudged up the steps and across the wooden porch before awkwardly opening the door. Stepping into the entry hall, she heard voices coming from the dining room. After easing the bags to the floor, she followed the voices to the dining room where Dirk, Tessa, her two boys and Aunt Dee sat, staring at a laptop.

"What's going on?"

"We're looking at our new house." Tessa pointed to the 3D image on the computer screen.

Moving behind her, Audrey peered at the image of a modern farmhouse with white vertical siding and a black roof. "Nice! One story or two?"

"One." Tessa clasped her hands together. "I love the front porch so we can enjoy that spectacular view." Tessa and Dirk had searched the ranch for just the right spot to build, but it was ultimately Dirk's dog, Molly, that led them to it.

"How'd the shopping go?" asked Aunt Dee.

"Good," said Audrey. "I could use some help unloading, though."

150   *Their Texas Christmas Redemption*

"In that case—" Aunt Dee stood "—Grayson and Bryce, why don't you come help us?"

When Audrey and her aunt had deposited the last two lamps in the spare room a short time later, Audrey said, "What's for supper?"

"Tessa and Dirk are taking the boys out for pizza and I'm havin' leftovers. Care to join me?"

Audrey's phone rang then. Pulling it from her pocket, she eyed the screen. "It's Tyler." She glanced at her aunt. "I wonder why he's calling."

"Well, answer it and find out." With a chuckle, her aunt turned and started back downstairs.

Audrey tapped the screen as she returned to her room. "Hey, Tyler."

"What are you doing?"

"I just got back from Houston."

"Ah. You must be worn out."

"What? No, I was shopping for the tent cabins. You know how jazzed I can get about stuff like that."

He chuckled. "In that case, would you care to join me for a campfire?"

"Great idea. This is perfect campfire weather." The words were out of her mouth before she could stop them.

"I was thinking the same thing. And since there's this nice firepit behind the cabin, maybe we could roast some hot dogs."

"Only if we can have s'mores for dessert." Why was she being so agreeable?

"Sorry, no chocolate, graham crackers or marshmallows down here."

"Oh, well, it just so happens that I have warehouse-size packages of all of the above." A token so their guests could enjoy the whole camping experience.

"Nice. So what do you say?"

How foolish was it that her heart raced as though the cutest boy in school had just asked her out? And while Tyler was definitely cute, he was still her ex—make that her friend.

"I need to change clothes. I'll be there in ten to fifteen."

She quickly traded her joggers for a pair of well-worn jeans, then donned a flannel shirt over the white T-shirt she already wore before retrieving her Ropers from the closet. Perched on the side of her bed, she shoved her feet into the boots. "It's just a casual supper with a friend, so don't read anything into Tyler's invitation," she said out loud.

"Did you say something?"

Audrey jerked her head up to discover Tessa standing in the doorway. "Oh, I was just talking to myself."

Her sister leaned against the door jamb. "We're going out for pizza. Want to come?"

"No, thank you. Tyler invited me to roast hot dogs over a campfire."

Tessa's brow lifted, along with the corners of her mouth. "That sounds cozy."

"You forget he has an infant. That does not equate to cozy."

"Oh, I don't know about that." Straightening, her sister strolled into the room. "What I do know is that the two of you have been spending a *lot* of time together—"

"Forced proximity." Audrey lifted her chin. "He's helping us out with the ranch, so I help him with Willow."

"Whatever the case, you seem to be getting along well." Her smug look was more than a little annoying.

Then again, Audrey had yet to tell Tessa about the miscarriage.

Standing, she said, "It's strictly a business arrangement."

"Oh, so this is a business dinner."

"Mom?" Grayson's voice echoed up the stairwell. "We're ready."

Her gaze still fixed on Audrey, Tessa hollered, "I'll be right there!"

Feeling as though she ought to throw her sister a bone, Audrey said, "Look, Tyler and I have made amends. It's a long story, which I promise to tell you later when we both have time. However, we are strictly friends."

Seemingly satisfied, Tessa nodded and turned

for the door. "Looks like Aunt Dee will have the house to herself for a change."

Something that hadn't happened since Tessa and her boys arrived at the end of May for summer break. Then Tessa had accepted a teaching position in Hope Crossing, and Dirk's proposal soon followed.

When Audrey pulled up to the cabin several minutes later, lamplight glowed inside. And when she stepped out of her SUV, gripping the handles of a brown paper sack containing the makings for s'mores, the endearing aroma of burning wood had her muscles relaxing.

She started toward the porch, until movement inside the cabin caused her steps to slow. Peering through the window, she watched Tyler cradle Willow in his arms, his gaze fixed on the child, his smile wide. Yet instead of feeling sorrow over what might have been, Audrey found herself thinking how blessed Willow was to have him in her life.

Tyler really had changed. He was still confident in ways that mattered, yet as a person, he was humbler. More compassionate.

Tearing her gaze away from the window, she continued onto the porch and knocked on the door.

"Who do you suppose that is, Willow?" Audrey heard him say, making her grin.

A second later the door opened, and the smile

Tyler sent her had warmth radiating through her entire being.

His gaze swept over her. "Well look who's gone country.'" Waggling his brows, he added, "I like it." He held the door wide, inviting her in with a nod.

She eyed his red-and-black buffalo check flannel. "And you're channeling your inner lumberjack."

"Of course. I had to split wood for the fire."

Amid the sounds of college football on TV, Audrey turned her attention to Willow. She caressed the baby's cheek. "And our little miss is pretty in pink." Her hand froze when she realized what she'd said. *Our.* As if Willow belonged to her and Tyler.

Rather than calling attention to her error, she turned her smile Tyler's way and held up the bag. "As promised, I brought dessert."

"Awesome. The fire and sticks are ready, so let's go."

With Willow content in her seat atop the nearby picnic table, Audrey slid her cold hot dog onto the pointed stick Tyler had fashioned with his pocketknife while he did the same. Then they held the sticks over the fire, watching as the flames lapped at the skin, causing the juices to drip.

"Browned or charred?" He glanced her way.

"How about somewhere in between?" She rotated her stick—then watched as the hot dog slid into the fire. "Oh, no!" She pouted. "My hot dog."

To his credit, Tyler didn't so much as grin. Instead, he reached for the package of franks and handed it to her. "It's alright. I've got plenty more."

"Thank you." Armed with another dog, she repeated the process, making sure she slid the stick well into the link before putting it into the fire. "Okay, let's try this again." She eyed Tyler's perfectly blackened dog as he reached for a bun. "Nice work."

"Thanks."

Returning her attention to her own, she saw it slipping once again. "No, no, no, no!" She turned the stick, hoping to avoid another disaster, but to no avail. "Doh!" Sulking again, she said, "And another one bites the dust."

This time, he did smile, though he tried to hide it. "Don't give up. We're gonna make this work."

"I don't understand. I've never had this happen with marshmallows."

This time, he slid the dog onto her stick, then remained at her side when she stuck it into the flames. "Lift the tip up a little bit."

"Like this?"

Evidently not, because his arm came around her. Placing his hand atop hers, he lowered the back end of the stick, putting it at more of an angle.

156 *Their Texas Christmas Redemption*

In that moment, it wasn't the hot dog that concerned her. Tyler's proximity had her heart racing. He smelled of smoke, spit-up and a hint of musk. A strange, yet oddly appealing, aroma.

"Alright, let's give it a turn." His breath was warm on her ear as he helped her manipulate the stick. "It's starting to char." He had yet to move.

And she hadn't, either. She'd forgotten how wonderful it felt to be in his embrace.

"I think it's good to go."

Turning, she found his face mere inches from her own. Her mouth went dry. "'Kay."

"Let me get you a bun." He stood then.

As the cool night air settled in around her, she chided herself for getting lost in the moment. He was only trying to help her, like any friend would do. Except he wasn't just any friend. He was a friend who'd once known her on an intimate level.

"Here you go."

Her cheeks burned as she took the bun from his hand. She stood, silently praying he would attribute her sudden blush to the fire and not his proximity.

Thankfully, after one hot dog, three s'mores and conversation about the barn, she felt much better.

Beside her, Tyler was holding Willow, though she was growing fussier by the minute, even refusing her bottle.

After dusting off her hands, Audrey held them out. "Here, let me see if I can get her to calm down." Taking hold of the child, she drew the blanket tighter and held her close.

Willow fell silent, staring up at Audrey, and Audrey thought her heart might burst.

"I guess we know who her favorite is." Tyler nudged her elbow with his.

"Only because she's been with you all day." She patted Willow's bottom as the infant's eyes fluttered closed.

Leaning back, he clasped his hands atop his flat stomach. "I was wondering..." His voice trailed off before he straightened. "How would you feel about me staying through Christmas Under the Stars. That way, I can help you with all the lights and setup and be available in case there are any problems that night."

When she kept silent, staring at the fire while she processed the possible implications of such a move, he took a deep breath and forged on.

"It'll also allow me to help you finish out the interiors of the tent cabins. I should have the last platform done Monday." He heaved a sigh. "Being here has been good for me. I'm not ready to let go of this—" He motioned to the darkened countryside. "That said, I understand if you don't want me around. I mean, I have monopolized the cabin."

"It's part of your payment, remember." She

found herself grappling with how eager she was to say yes. Having him here for so long could be dangerous. To her anyway. Because the more time she spent with Tyler, the more she realized that while the best parts of him remained intact, the not-so-good parts had been transformed into the kind of man she could envision spending the rest of her life with.

Chapter Ten

"I'm so excited," Audrey all but squealed from the passenger seat of his truck late the next Saturday afternoon. She was convinced they needed to get started hanging lights for Christmas Under the Stars—which was still three weeks away—so Tyler had agreed to help her, even though the area wouldn't have electricity until next week.

The clear November sky promised another hour or so of daylight as Tyler shifted his truck into Park near the completed tent cabin platforms, his gaze drifting to his enthusiastic sidekick.

"This has been such a good week." She practically beamed beneath her Get Your Jingle On ball cap, while her ponytail swayed back and forth over a T-shirt that sported a smiling red-nosed reindeer.

"Yes, it has. A very productive one, at that."

Not only had Tyler finished the last platform and begun attaching the tent poles, Bruce Hendricks and his crew from North Texas had rolled in like a small army Monday morning and immediately set to work on the barn.

Over four days, they'd built cribs made of four-foot wood blocks to the support steel beams they later threaded through each corner. Then they ran cables to square the barn before jacking the entire structure five feet off the ground so concrete footers could be poured. And it would remain there until the footers were set and the crew returned to lower the barn late next week, allowing Tyler and Dirk some much-needed time to focus solely on the tent cabins.

Though for all the activity, Tyler routinely found himself plagued by memories of what had happened around that campfire last weekend. Helping Audrey with that hot dog had seemed like such an innocent gesture. Instead, it reminded him of how perfectly she fit in his embrace—as though God had crafted her especially for him. And how Tyler had taken that precious gift for granted.

It humbled him yet again. And made him determined to prove to Audrey that he was no longer that man. Even if he had to hang a gazillion Christmas lights a thousand times over. And if the surplus of boxes he'd seen back at the ranch house were any indication, he might end up doing just that.

"Now it's time to start working on Christmas." Audrey's enthusiasm grew with each word. "I'm glad Tessa offered to watch Willow. Not that she's a bother, but it'll allow us to work uninterrupted."

"Agreed. Now, let's do it."

They exited the cab to meet at the back of the pickup. Tyler lowered the tailgate as Audrey unfurled the sketch she'd drawn of the area, using colored pencils, no less.

Removing his Rangers ball cap, he scratched his head, suddenly feeling rather overwhelmed. "There's a lot more stuff in this drawing than what we purchased at the home improvement center." He tugged his cap back on.

"Some of it is stuff Aunt Dee already had." Audrey was very matter-of-fact. "I've also been doing a *ton* of online shopping."

Peering down at her, he felt a brow lifting. "You don't say."

Despite the pink blooming on her cheeks, she raised her chin. "There are a lot of areas around the ranch to decorate this year. Not only here—" she swept a hand through the air "—but the ranch house, the cabin, the bunkhouse and, of course, the main entrance." Perching a hand on one hip, she continued, "Did you know they make all sorts of solar and battery-operated lights and decorations? And they're not that expensive."

"Do tell?"

Waving him off, she said, "Oh, hush. It's a business expense."

He couldn't help chuckling. Did she have any

idea how cute she was? He'd always found her enthusiasm contagious. It was why he'd agreed to deck out their home in Fort Worth. He'd have walked over hot coals to make her vision come true. Yet he hadn't been man enough to open up about his past and stick by her when she'd needed him most.

Further proof Audrey is too good for you.

He shook off the wayward thought. He couldn't change the past, but he could prove that *he'd* changed.

Smoothing a hand over her drawing atop the tailgate, Audrey continued. "So the bonfire is going to be right there." After designating the position on the map, she turned to point toward the grassy area behind them, enveloped by the large circular drive. "I'd like to have the food and drink tables closer to the cabins—" she twisted that way "—where we'll have easy access to water, as well as electricity for lighting, slow cookers and stuff like that. So we'll need to hang a fair amount of globe light strands over that area."

"Like we did in our backyard?" The small fenced space with beautiful landscaping as well as sitting and eating areas had always been one of their favorite places to entertain.

"Exactly." Her eyes sparkled as though recalling happy memories. At least he hoped so.

He looked from the space to her drawing and back again. "I'll need to come up with something to drape the lights from. The trees are too far apart, but I can build some posts."

Placing a hand on his forearm, she smiled up at him, the contact making his heart long for things he had no right to expect. "See, this is why I need you. You take my harebrained ideas and make them a beautiful reality."

What he wouldn't give to have *her* be his beautiful reality again.

You had your chance. And you blew it—bigtime.

Shaking off the inner chastisement, he said, "Okay, so why don't you walk me around and show me what you're going to want where so I can get a mental picture. Then we can start wrapping some of the tree trunks with lights, since that can be rather time-consuming."

After walking around the area, going over her notes and discussing what would look best where, they returned to the truck to retrieve several boxes of miniature white lights. Then they went to one of the oak trees near the platforms.

While he started opening the boxes, Audrey scurried to the nearest platform. After setting something small and black atop the wood, she pulled out her phone. "Before we get to work, we need a little something to get us into the Christmas spirit."

As if Christmas spirit had ever been a problem for Audrey.

Soon, Andy Williams was blaring across the pasture, heralding the most wonderful time of the year.

When she joined him again, he said, "You realize Thanksgiving is almost two weeks away."

One brow arched. "Since when did that ever stop me?"

He laughed. "Never." Audrey loved Christmas. And he loved her enthusiasm. Had missed it. "I assume your Christmas tree still goes up before Thanksgiving?"

Shrugging, she said, "At my place, yes. We'll see what Aunt Dee has to say. Though I will do my best to win her over." She opened a box, pulled out the bundle of lights and began removing the twist ties. "What about you?"

He wasn't sure how to respond. He hadn't had a Christmas tree since she left. Because it would only remind him of her. Most Christmas things did.

"Hello?" Head cocked, she eyed him. "Anybody home?"

He may as well be forthcoming, because she wouldn't give up until she got her answer. "I don't usually do a tree."

Her gaze narrowed. "What do you mean by 'usually'?"

"Okay, more like never."

Her eyes went wide. "But you always loved Christmas."

Because she was the one who'd shown him how wonderful Christmas could be. Without her...

"I'm too busy with work." Hoping to change the subject, he said, "Let's get started on these lights. I'll wind, you check the spacing."

"Hold on, let me get an extension cord." She stopped. "Wait, where's an outlet?"

"The electrician hasn't been out here yet, but there's one in my truck. I'll show you."

Once the lights were illuminated, they returned to the tree and set to work.

Standing on her tiptoes to reach the lights where the tree trunk V'd, Audrey said, "I guess you'll be here for Thanksgiving, huh?"

As he worked the strand toward the main trunk, his movements slowed. It sounded as though the thought had just occurred to her. And judging by her tone, he got the feeling she did not want him invading her holiday.

Lifting his chin, he continued winding the lights around the trunk, determined to ignore the twinge of disappointment withering his insides. "It looks that way. It'll be a nice opportunity for Willow and me to hang around the cabin, watch football and eat pumpkin pie."

"Oh."

Wait, why did she sound disappointed?

She watched him now. "You mean you're not going to join us at the house?"

Still circling the tree, making sure things were taut, all while taking care not to trip over her, he said, "I don't make a habit of showing up to events I'm not invited to."

"What do you mean not invited?" Sounding almost indignant, she added, "You know Aunt Dee is going to expect you to join us." Crouching, she resumed adjusting the spacing. "Though I should warn you that Meredith and Kendall will likely be there, as well."

He cringed. Kendall, the baby of the family, would be okay. She was pretty chill. However, Meredith, the eldest of the four Hunt sisters, might take issue with him. After all, he was Audrey's *ex*-husband.

"Let me do us both a favor and just cut to the chase." Stopping beside her, he stared down at her. "Do *you* want me there?"

Slowly straightening, she kept her gaze locked on his.

He didn't flinch.

"Why would you ask such a thing? Of course I do."

He hoped she hadn't heard the air rushing out of his lungs.

Returning to the task at hand, she added, "After all, we are friends. Besides, I found the most adorable outfit for Willow."

Tyler felt as though he'd been punched in the gut. How could he have been so ignorant? So foolish as to think he might be able to win Audrey's heart again? There was no spark between them. He'd only imagined it. It was Willow Audrey had fallen in love with. Not him.

"Knock, knock." Tessa's voice was accompanied by two raps on Audrey's bedroom door early Thursday evening, right before she cracked it open.

Sitting on her bed, pillows tucked behind her as she leaned against the headboard, Audrey sighed. "Come in."

"Well, nothing like a hearty welcome." Tessa closed the door behind her. "I thought you'd be bouncing all over the place now that the barn's been put back to rights." She eased onto the edge of the bed. "So what gives? You've been moping all week. That's not like you."

Setting her iPad aside, Audrey grabbed a throw pillow and hugged it against her tummy. Tessa was right. Despite the barn people returning today to lower the structure onto its new footings, Audrey had been in a funk most of the week.

"Tyler has been acting strange since we worked on the lights Saturday. He stayed away completely on Sunday, and he's bowed out of suppers here at the house every night this week. He just picks up Willow and goes back to the cabin." She even took Willow out to the tent cabins when Tyler and Dirk were working there on Tuesday, but she ended up talking to Dirk while Tyler kept working.

"Did you two have an argument or something?"

She shook her head. "No." But it stung. Brought back memories of how he'd behaved after her miscarriage.

Cocking her head, Tessa said, "Sounds like you miss him."

Audrey drew in a long breath, not wanting to admit it, but knowing it was true. "I guess I do, kind of. He was always fun to be around. We had a lot of good times together. That's why it hurt so much when he turned away after the miscarriage." She'd filled Tessa in on the real reason behind her divorce not long after telling Aunt Dee. "And this kinda feels the same way."

Tessa eased down on the side of the bed. "Do you still have feelings for Tyler?"

Audrey shrugged. "He's changed—in a good way."

"How so?"

"For starters, he's a man of faith." She lifted a shoulder. "The things I admired most about him—he's outgoing, fun to be with, attentive—are still there. Except now he's more genuine. Instead of trying to cover up the scars from his past for fear someone might see his brokenness, he's willing to be real with me."

"God can move mountains. Sounds like you've both changed for the better."

Audrey hugged the pillow tighter. "So why is he avoiding me? And how do I find out what's going on with him?"

Tessa's brows shot up. "Seriously? You two divorced because of a lack of communication. Now you're going to let the same thing come between your friendship—or whatever it is that's brewing between y'all?"

Audrey sighed. "But how do I do that when he won't talk to me?"

"Oh, good grief." Tessa shot off the bed. "Go talk to the guy and ask *him* what's wrong."

Worrying her lip, Audrey said, "You make it sound so simple."

"And you're acting as though it's rocket science."

"I never was good at science."

"Audrey, get off your bottom and go down to the cabin and ask Tyler why he's avoiding you. Even if you don't like his answer, at least you'll have one."

With a sigh, Audrey threw her legs over the side of the bed and stood. "Will you pray for me?"

"You know I will." Tessa hugged her. "Now, go!" She waved her on. "Though you might want a sweater. It's kind of chilly outside."

Audrey checked the time. It was just after eight. Tyler should still be up.

After slipping her feet into her sneakers, she bounded down the stairs.

"Where you goin'?" Aunt Dee stood at her bedroom door.

"Tessa will fill you in." She opened the door. "I'll be back soon."

The cool night air settled around her as she bounded down the front steps and hurried to her SUV. A minute and a half later, she was pulling up in front of the cabin.

She started to open the door, only to find herself second-guessing her decision to rush down here. One what-if after another raced through her mind.

Go down to the cabin and ask Tyler why he's avoiding you. Even if you don't like his answer, at least you'll have one.

Tessa was right. Better to know than to be left wondering.

Stepping into the night air, she continued onto the porch, the sound of a football game spilling from inside. Tyler liked his football.

With a deep breath, she knocked on the door. Seconds later, she saw him peer through the window before moving to the door.

When it opened, he said, "Audrey? What are you doing here?" He was wearing gray sweatpants and a black T-shirt with a spit-up stain on the shoulder. Something she found oddly endearing. "Willow is already down for the night."

"Good. That means we can talk uninterrupted." She arched a brow. "May I come in?"

After a moment, he waved her inside.

"Mmm, it smells good in here." She looked at him. "Have you been baking?"

Blushing, he said, "I don't think microwave brownies can be considered baking."

"Oooh...got any left?" Chocolate always helped calm her nerves.

"They're from a mix." He gestured to a small pan on the counter. "But help yourself."

So she did. Okay, maybe she was stalling.

He watched while she nibbled. "Why are you here?"

She swallowed. "Because I need to talk to you about something. Have you got any milk?"

His expression turned wary. "Yeah. Help yourself."

After retrieving a juice glass from the cupboard, she grabbed the 1% from the refrigerator and poured a small amount.

Arms crossed, he said, "What do you need to talk to me about?"

She chugged the milk, rinsed the cup and set it in the sink. Then she looked him in the eye. "We haven't had a real conversation since we worked on the lights Saturday. You pick up Willow and leave instead of hanging around for supper. It feels like you're avoiding me, and I want to know why."

Scratching his head, he sighed. "You have Willow for seven to eight hours a day. Isn't that enough?"

Her gaze instinctively narrowed. "What does that have to do with us? I thought we were friends, yet you've barely spoken to me since we worked on the lights."

His biceps bulging, he shook his head. "I got the hint, alright."

Okay, now she was even more confused. "What hint? What are you talking about?"

"That you're more interested in spending time with Willow than me."

"What? You asked me if I wanted you at Thanksgiving and I said yes."

He nodded. "Then you started talking about some outfit for Willow, as if the only reason you'd want me there was so you could play dress-up with her."

Audrey had not been expecting that. It was almost as if he was jealous. "Tyler, you and Willow are a package deal. Yes, I enjoy my time with her, and yes, her cute little outfits are fun, but I like being with you, too. Getting to know the man you've become."

He stared at her, the lines in his brow softening. "Y-you do?"

"Yes. Spending time with you, working as a

team again has brought back a lot of good memories. After years of dwelling on the bad, I needed to be reminded that things weren't always that way. I'm sorry if I sounded as though I was only interested in Willow. Truth is, I enjoy spending time with her handsome uncle, too."

He pulled in a deep breath and let it go, his body seemingly deflating. "I'm sorry. I behaved like a jerk."

Squinting up at him, she said, "Does this mean you're not mad at me anymore?"

His gaze locked with hers. "That is correct."

"When I was talking to Tessa earlier tonight, she pointed out that it was a lack of communication that tore our marriage apart." Lifting a shoulder, she said, "Going forward, do you suppose we could be the kind of friends who are open and truthful with each other?"

He glanced away. "Well, you did see me cry." He looked at her again, a shy smile pulling at his lips. "So I think we can do that."

"Good." She turned toward the television. "Who's playing?"

"Chiefs and the Raiders. You still a Mahomes fan?"

"He's from Texas. Of course I am."

"In that case, care to join me?"

She grinned. "I thought you'd never ask."

Chapter Eleven

It was almost dark when Tyler climbed into his truck Friday evening, calling it quits on the tent cabins for a couple of days. He and Dirk had made some substantial progress this week, working from dawn til dusk. And the longer hours had paid off. Siding, windows and a door had been added to the facades, the metal tent frames secured to the platforms and the canvases draped. Then siding was added to the lower third of the sides and back to help insulate and keep bugs out. Finally, back doors were installed, essentially making the cabins dried in. The only things left to do on the exterior were to add metal roofs to the front porches, as well as handrails on the porches and decks.

For the better part of the week, Tyler had welcomed the longer hours. They'd given him an excuse to skip out on meals with Audrey and her family and spend his evenings with Willow at the cabin. But after Audrey's unexpected visit last night, he was eager to get back to the routine he'd come to enjoy more than he ever anticipated.

Seemed he still had a lot to learn when it came to relationships. Because whenever he felt as though one was threatened—whether perceived or real—his instinct was to retreat. Thankfully, Audrey hadn't been afraid to call him out.

Now he was looking forward to the weekend and spending time with her.

He propelled his pickup along the dirt road that had him passing by the newly positioned barn. The concrete people would be back the week after Thanksgiving to prep for the barn's new foundation, expanding its existing footprint, and would hopefully pour the concrete shortly after that. Which would make Audrey happy, bolstering her hopes for the venue's construction to begin in January. Too bad he wouldn't be there to be a part of things.

Shaking off the unwanted thought, he continued to the ranch house. Lights glowed from inside the old home, and as he stepped into the evening air, a slight chill had him debating whether he should grab the flannel shirt he'd worn early this morning from the back seat.

Nah.

He rounded the front of his vehicle and was approaching the steps when he noticed something different. Evergreen garland had been draped from the porch rails and adorned with miniature white lights and substantial red bows, adding an inviting glow to the space. Audrey's doing, no doubt. The woman loved Christmas. And that was only one small part of what made her so special.

After climbing the steps, he knocked on the door. A few moments later, Tessa opened it.

"Hi, Tyler."

"How's it going?"

"Pretty good. Especially now that the weekend is here." She smiled, but didn't appear to be in any hurry to let him inside. "I'm supposed to let you know that Audrey took Willow down to the cabin and said for you to meet them there."

"Oh." Why hadn't Audrey contacted him? He pulled his phone from his pocket to double-check. Nope, nothing. "In that case, thanks for the info. I'll see you later." With a wave, he retreated to his truck, curious as to why she'd gone to the cabin without telling him. Not that he minded. Maybe she needed something for Willow. Had she run out of diapers? Still, he would've thought she'd told him to go straight there.

Whatever the case, it didn't erase the fact that he would finally get to spend time with her again. Simply picking up Willow and going home this week had definitely left him in a funk. Sure, he'd been annoyed, believing Willow was the only reason Audrey was hanging around, but he'd missed her, too. A lot. Though he wasn't quite sure what to make of that.

When he pulled up to the cabin, only the kitchen light was on inside, making him wonder if, maybe, she was preparing supper for them. That had his smile growing.

Grabbing his cooler, he exited the truck, feeling lighter than he had all week. He'd barely stepped onto the front porch when the front door opened and Audrey came outside, one hand in the air.

"Stop right there."

He froze. "Why? Is something wrong?"

"No. I just don't want you to come inside yet." Her gaze narrowing, she said, "Close your eyes."

Despite the door barely being ajar, something aromatic drifted through the crack, awakening his appetite. "Uh, you are aware this is where I live—for the time being anyway?"

"Yes, now close your eyes."

"Why?" Goose bumps peppered his bare arms as the cool air settled around him.

Her exasperation seemed to grow as she perched her hands on her hips. "Because I said so."

Though he wanted to continue harassing her, acquiescing to her demand was probably a better idea. "Alright, they're closed."

"Okay, now stay right there *with* your eyes closed until I tell you to come in."

"Yes, ma'am." The door closed but didn't latch,

allowing him to hear her soft footfalls against the wooden floor inside, as well as Willow's cooing. Then he caught another whiff of whatever it was he'd smelled before, making his stomach growl.

Finally, he heard her steps getting closer. Then the door creaked open. "You may come in now."

When he opened his eyes, light spilled through the windows. Then he stepped inside, his eyes widening as he took in the sight before him.

On the far side of the fireplace, a slim Christmas tree with white lights, red-and-black buffalo check ribbon, and silver and red ornaments glowed in the corner. The mantel was also adorned with evergreen, lights and pinecones, while two stockings—one red-and-black buffalo check and the other white-and-gray buffalo check with *Willow* written on the white fur in silver lettering—dangled from its edge.

For a moment, his heart stopped beating, only to pound a moment later. The absolute wonder of it all had him feeling like a kid on Christmas morning. Not that he knew how that felt. But he'd spent years imagining.

He shoved a hand through his hair. "What is all this?"

Now holding Willow, Audrey moved beside him. "I couldn't bear the thought of you not having a Christmas tree, so this is an early Christmas present for you and Willow." He started to interrupt her, but she held up a hand. "I know,

Thanksgiving is still six days away, and you'll probably be gone before Christmas, but selfishly, I wanted to see how it all looked." Admiring her handiwork, she added, "I saved all the boxes so you can take everything back to Fort Worth and set it up there. Oh, and all the ornaments are plastic, so you won't have to worry about Willow breaking any of them. Later, that is. When she's mobile."

He stared at her, wondering how he could have let her go. For a moment, he contemplated telling her why he hadn't had a tree since she left Fort Worth. But then, that might make her feel bad. He didn't want to dampen the festive mood after she'd gone to all this trouble. On the contrary, he was flabbergasted that she'd gone out of her way to do all of this for him and Willow, no matter how much Audrey loved Christmas.

Blinking away the uncharacteristic moisture suddenly blurring his vision, he said, "It's beautiful." Just like her. "We're going to have to start calling you Santa's sneaky little helper." Then, without thinking, he slipped an arm around her shoulders, pulled her close and planted a kiss on her temple. "Thank you." Man, did she smell good.

He released her and she looked up at him wearing a lopsided smile, her eyes wide.

"I'm glad you like it."

"So what's that I smell cooking?"

"Roasted pork tenderloin with sweet potatoes and some apple dumplings for dessert, heavy on the cinnamon."

"Wow!" And after the way he'd treated her this week. "What's the occasion?"

"No occasion. It just sounded like a delicious fall-ish meal."

"It smells great. When can we dig in?"

"As soon as you get cleaned up."

"In that case..." After dropping a kiss atop Willow's downy head, he went to the bathroom and washed up before climbing the stairs to the loft for a fresh shirt, all the while wondering what it would be like to come home to a scene like this every night.

Audrey would be a wonderful mother. The way she loved Willow and took such good care of her never ceased to amaze him.

Except he and Audrey weren't a couple. The decorations were for him to take home. A home Audrey no longer resided in. A home that felt lifeless without her. A home he'd soon be selling so he and Willow could start a new life somewhere else. Without Audrey.

"I can't believe the holidays are almost here." At the bunkhouse late Monday morning, Audrey peered into the carrier perched atop the pullout sofa, pleased to find Willow still sound asleep.

Now, if she'd just stay that way until they finished prepping the place for their next round of guests.

"I know." Tessa descended the stairs from the sleeping loft. Her boys were hanging out with Dirk and Tyler today. "Even better, not only do I have this week off school, when I go back there will be only three weeks until Christmas break." She poked a thumb over her shoulder. "Everything is ready to go up there."

"Thanks." Audrey had managed to break away from Tyler, Willow and a lazy football afternoon at the cabin yesterday to run over here long enough to strip the beds and spray sanitizer on the mattresses after their guests checked out.

Beside her sister now, she said, "Do you want to vacuum up there, or should I?" The space with knotty pine walls and ceiling was the only area of the bunkhouse with carpet, but it sure helped with noise control.

"I'll do it." Tessa palmed her insulated tumbler from the small wooden dining table. "Just as soon as I finish my coffee break." With a wink, she took a swig.

"In that case, I think I'll join you." Grabbing her pink tumbler, she touched it to Tessa's blue one. "Cheers."

After a long draw, Tessa ran a finger over her cup's lid. "So, it appears you and Tyler have picked up right where you left off since your impromptu visit Thursday night."

Shifting from one foot to the other, Audrey said, "And where was that?"

Tessa's hazel eyes met hers. "Spending as much time together as possible."

"Oh, come on, Tess. He's helping me prep for Christmas Under the Stars." On Saturday, they'd decorated the ranch entrance, not to mention added lights to some of the trees around the ranch house before enjoying another campfire. Sunday had been pretty laid back, though, with only church and football.

"Yes—" her sister perched a fist on her hip "—but if you'll recall, Dirk spent a lot of time helping me remove that nasty old paneling from the living and dining rooms to get to the shiplap. So you can't convince me there's not something more to the situation." She started to take a drink, then paused. "I mean, you decorated the cabin for him."

While she was scowling at her sister, Audrey was smiling inside. The look on Tyler's face Friday night had been worth any amount of effort. The childlike wonder in his eyes had to be one of the sweetest things she'd ever seen. But what she couldn't quite understand was how a simple kiss—which wasn't even on the lips—could have such an effect on her. Just thinking about it had chill bumps peppering her arms. Thankfully, she was wearing three-quarter-length sleeves.

"Let me ask you something." Head cocked,

her second-eldest sister watched her intently. "If you had a second chance with Tyler, would you take it?"

Still holding her cup, Audrey took a thoughtful breath. "I honestly don't know. I mean, I can see that he's changed, and we're definitely friends. Still, even though I now know the bigger story behind his actions, I'm just not sure I could ever fully trust him with my heart." She started to take a drink, then added, "Besides, his life is in Fort Worth, while mine is here."

She took a sip, eager to change the subject. Lowering her tumbler, she eyed her sister. "Want to know a secret?"

Tessa's eyes lit up. "Oooh, yes, please."

"I'm planning to adopt a child, preferably a baby."

"Whoa! When did you decide this?"

"I've been contemplating it for the last year or so. It's kind of why I wanted to live here at the ranch. And watching Willow while settling into my role here has given me a glimpse of what my life might be like when I become a mother. You know, juggling work and family."

"Oh, I'm very familiar with that."

God willing, Audrey's dream of being a mom would, one day, come to fruition. Perhaps, once things settled down in the spring, she'd be able to initiate the process.

A knock at the door had them both turning that way as their aunt pushed it open.

"Whatcha know, girls?" Still on the porch, she toed out of her boots.

With a nod toward their aunt, Tessa said, "Does she know?"

Aunt Dee stepped inside and started toward them, her gaze darting between Tessa and Audrey. "Know what?"

"About my intention to adopt."

The woman's shoulders dropped. "I'm glad you finally decided to spill the beans. You know how I hate keepin' secrets."

Willow began to fuss then.

"Uh-oh." Audrey returned her cup to the table.

"I'll git her." Aunt Dee waved her off as she crossed the short distance to peer into the carrier. "Hello there, sweet girl."

Looking at Tessa, Audrey said, "Once we're finished in here, I want to add some lights and garlands to the porch." She pointed that way. "Make things look nice and festive for our guests."

"Good idea."

Amid the aromas of coffee and lemony freshness, Aunt Dee sashayed toward them with a contented Willow. "Baby girl, you're gittin' heavier by the day."

Audrey kissed Willow's cheek. "Can you believe she'll be four months old in a little over a week?" Tyler had already scheduled a checkup at the urgent care in Hope Crossing. One that would include immunizations.

She cringed at the thought. And supposed she ought to anticipate Tyler's niece being a little out of sorts for a day or so afterward. Yet another tidbit she needed to tuck away for future reference.

Aunt Dee smiled down at Willow. She was definitely enjoying having a baby around. Audrey prayed she could make that a long-term thing.

Looking from Audrey to Tessa, their aunt said, "I stopped by to check on the fellas. While Grayson and Bryce played outside, Dirk and Tyler were busy framin' all the bathrooms. Dirk says the plumber and electrician will be out tomorrow mornin'. Once they're gone, our boys'll Sheetrock those bathroom walls, then he and Tyler will concentrate on settin' cabinets and layin' the floor in cabin number two Wednesday. That way they can take the rest of the week off."

She looked at Audrey then, obviously sensing she was about to protest. "Come Monday, you'll be able to start movin' stuff into that cabin. Tyler will work around you, if needed, but he'll still have plenty of stuff to do in the other cabins."

Relaxing, Audrey said, "In that case, I'll get deliveries scheduled for next week."

Swaying back and forth as she cradled Willow in her arms, their aunt grinned. "My dream is finally comin' true." She looked from Tessa to

Audrey. "I can't tell you how tickled I am. And to have y'all workin' alongside me on this is more than I ever expected." Her voice cracked.

"Aww," the sisters said collectively before moving on either side of their aunt for a group hug.

"We're blessed to have you, Aunt Dee," said Tessa.

"And thankful you're allowing us to play a small role in fulfilling those dreams," Audrey added.

The older woman sniffed. "I just have one question."

Pulling away, they watched her expectantly.

Her blue gaze darted between them. "Which one of you is gonna brave a trip to the grocery store to do our Thanksgiving shopping?"

"I'll volunteer," said Audrey. "Who all's going to be there?"

"Well, all of us, as well as the four fellas. Meredith said she'd come out, but Kendall's questionable."

"What about Gentry?" Tessa asked. "I haven't seen him around for a while, except on the ranch."

Her aunt waved off the comment. "Nah, he's got a girlfriend."

"Girlfriend?" Tessa eyed Audrey, who shrugged, not knowing any more than her sister. "I thought the two of you—I mean, you always seemed to be together."

Their aunt nodded. "We considered somethin'

more but decided it might ruin our friendship." Shaking her head, she added, "He's not my type, anyway."

Aunt Dee had a type? That was news to Audrey. "What is your type?"

Suddenly thoughtful, the woman cocked her head. "Actually, I prefer someone a little more intellectual." She glared at them. "That is, *if* I was lookin' for a man. Which I'm not."

Chapter Twelve

Thanksgiving at Aunt Dee's was like revisiting a cherished memory. Her dining room table was where Tyler had enjoyed his first *real* Thanksgiving seven years ago. The kind of gathering that had so much food you couldn't fit it all on the table that was surrounded by a large family.

When Tyler and Audrey were married, Tyler would start counting down the days as soon as the calendar turned to November. He and Audrey would make the trip from Fort Worth to Legacy Ranch every year. Until his invitation was permanently rescinded.

Thanks to a temporary reprieve, this year he'd once again been blessed to enjoy Thanksgiving around Aunt Dee's table. And while the food had been every bit as delicious as he remembered, it wasn't the only part of the day he'd found himself looking forward to.

The long walks he and Audrey always took after their big meal had been filled with laughter and intimate conversation as they discussed their hopes and dreams for the impending holiday season, as well as their future. It was on one of those walks they'd made the decision to start building a family.

Parked on the leather sofa in the ranch house family room, his belly still bloated from today's feast, he hoped Audrey might agree to another of those walks he remembered so fondly. And now that the Cowboys game had ended in victory, she was even more apt to be in an agreeable mood.

As if reading his mind, she said, "This calls for a celebration." With Willow in one arm, Audrey stood from her spot opposite him on the sofa and made her way across the area rug and tile floor, before continuing into the adjacent kitchen.

Relaxing in her overstuffed recliner, Aunt Dee said, "What kinda celebration?"

"Another slice of pecan pie, of course," Audrey tossed over her shoulder.

Patting her own stomach, Dee shook her head. "How could you possibly have room?"

Audrey stopped alongside the lemon-yellow counter. "Aunt Dee, there is always room for more pie."

"Ugh." Meredith—who'd arrived from Houston yesterday—frowned, hugging her own abdomen. "I couldn't eat any more if I had to."

While Dirk, Tessa and the boys had joined them for lunch, they'd left to visit his parents as soon as the dishes were cleaned up.

Now armed with the remote control, Aunt Dee said, "Anyone up for a Christmas movie?"

"Yes, please." Audrey's eldest sister smiled from the loveseat.

"I sure wish Kendall coulda come today." With a sigh, Dee pointed the clicker at the television, changing it to one of those channels that had been showing nothing but holiday romance movies since October.

"Did she have to work?" Meredith frowned.

"No, she's got an early flight to Colorado tomorrow for some culinary event with a bunch of fancy chefs. The *chef* she works under asked her to join him." Hands splayed atop the arms of her chair, she added, "We'll have to give her a call later."

Still hoping he could talk Audrey into that walk, Tyler pushed off the couch. "Excuse me, ladies." He followed the path Audrey had taken into the kitchen where countless aromas still hung in the air.

Coming alongside her as she bit into a sliver of pie, Willow at her shoulder, he leaned against the counter. "I was thinking about taking Willow for a walk. We could both use some fresh air." No, he was not above using his niece as a ploy. "Would you care to join us?"

Wearing a white baseball shirt with green sleeves and *Is it Christmas yet?* emblazoned in bold red lettering, her hair in a messy bun, Audrey eyed him. "Good idea." She gestured to the morsel of pie still in her hand. "It'll give me an opportunity to work off some of this food so I'll have room for more."

He couldn't help chuckling as she tossed the last bit into her mouth. "It's a good thing Thanksgiving only comes once a year." Breaking off a small piece of pumpkin bread for himself, he said, "Let me get the sling ready and I can carry Willow."

A few minutes later, they stepped onto the front porch and breathed in the pleasant late November air. With temperatures in the low sixties and plenty of sunshine, it felt very fall-like. If only there was some fall color. But that was a rarity in this part of Texas.

"Where would you like to go?" she asked as they descended the porch steps.

"How about the barn? I like that peaceful little pond over there."

"I do, too," she said as they started down the gravel drive. "Come spring, we'll need to clean up that entire area—trim the trees, do some landscaping. That way, there'll be a show-stopping view from the backside of the barn. Not to mention a great backdrop for wedding photos."

"Most definitely." Eyeing the web of tree limbs stretching over their heads, he absently patted Willow's bottom, a sudden hollow feeling in his chest. He'd be long gone by then. Probably settling into a new home in a neighborhood where the houses were only feet apart instead of miles. That was, if he ever found the right place.

Every night after putting Willow to bed, he'd settle in with his laptop and peruse the listings in various areas around Fort Worth—existing homes as well as new subdivisions. Yet every time he'd stumble onto something that looked promising, he'd discover some aspect that was less than appealing and end up closing the computer.

Shaking off his frustration, he glanced Audrey's way. "I guess now that Thanksgiving's over, you're ready to go full bore on Christmas, huh?"

Her smile widened. "You know me well, Tyler. Thankfully, except for the tent cabins and the Christmas Under the Stars area which we'll tackle next week, the outdoor decorations are all done." She nudged him with her elbow. "Thanks to you."

He felt his chest puffing. "Team Caldwell comes through again." Too bad it was only temporary.

Willow sneezed, causing their steps to halt as both he and Audrey turned their attention to her. The baby merely blinked and smiled up at them.

Audrey caressed Willow's cheek. "She is so cute."

"Takes after her uncle."

Lifting a brow, Audrey peered up at him. "Yes, she does."

Wait. Did she just say he was cute?

Giving himself a mental fist bump, he followed when she began walking again, a bit more spring in his step.

With gravel beneath their footfalls, Audrey said, "I've been meaning to ask you, how's the house hunt going?"

As reality again reared its ugly head, he said, "Not near as well as I'd hoped." He sighed. "To be honest, I don't even know what I'm looking for. I mean, just when I find something I think might work, I learn about some restriction or something else that has me ruling it out. It's driving me bonkers."

"I'm sorry." She sent him a sympathetic gaze. "I didn't realize it had become such a struggle."

"I never imagined buying a house could be so difficult. I look, but then when I try to anticipate the future—things like schools—I get overwhelmed and throw up my hands. It's becoming a vicious circle."

She settled a hand on his elbow, causing him to stop. Not to mention induce a sudden awareness. And the tenderness in her eyes wasn't helping. "First, have you prayed about this?"

"Daily."

"Would you prefer new construction or existing?"

"I'm open to either. You of all people know I have no problem renovating."

"Ah, but will you have the time to do such a project now that you have Willow?"

"Good point." He threw a hand up in the air. "See what I mean?"

"Tyler, you know this is not insurmountable."

He glanced her way. "It sometimes feels that way, though." Because, after spending the last seven-plus weeks at the ranch, city life in general held little appeal.

She stared up at him for a long moment, her gaze narrowing slightly, as though she was contemplating something. Cocking her head, she reached for his hand. "What if I did some searching for you? I mean, once upon a time, I had a knack for finding people's dream homes. Perhaps I could help you and Willow find yours. Gratis, of course."

His fingers closed around hers. "You'd really do that?"

"Sure. I mean, after all you've done for us here at the ranch, it's the least I can do." Her eyes met and held his. "It would be my pleasure to help you and Willow find your dream house."

Her nearness coupled with the sincerity in her gaze and the feel of her fingers entwined with his robbed him of all common sense. He stepped closer, cupping her cheek with his free hand, reveling in the softness of her skin.

Their eyes locked, and he could see a wealth of emotion swimming in those chestnut depths of hers. Oh, how he wanted to kiss her. To taste the sweetness of her lips once again.

He leaned closer.

Then Willow began to cry.

Audrey took a giant step backward, her cheeks pink. "She's probably hungry. We should go back to the house."

Audrey wasn't sure what was worse. That Tyler had almost kissed her, or that she'd wanted him to.

Despite trying to remain calm, cool and collected, she was certain her cheeks were flaming. What had come over her? First she grabbed hold of his hand, then she offered to help him find his perfect home—and then they almost kissed.

Thank goodness for Willow. Her little outburst had been nothing less than a divine interruption.

It was almost dark by the time they climbed the steps at the ranch house after a virtually silent walk back, the only discussion revolving around the weather. Now Audrey fought to regain an air of calm. Because if Aunt Dee suspected there was anything going on between Audrey and Tyler, Audrey would never hear the end of it.

She'd just reached for the door when Tyler said, "I think I'll just grab Willow's backpack and head on back to the cabin."

The comment had her wondering if he was feeling regret or disappointment.

"I understand." Nothing like your ex-wife throwing herself at you.

Inside, Willow whimpered as they continued through the entry hall.

"Why don't you let me fix her a bottle first?" Audrey said over her shoulder.

"Good idea. Thanks."

In the kitchen, Audrey retrieved a clean bottle from beside the sink and turned on the water.

"I'm glad y'all are back." Lowering the footrest on her recliner, her aunt stood and started toward them. "Watchin' this movie reminded me of somethin'."

Audrey turned off the water and grabbed the container of formula. "What's that?" After adding the powder to the water, she gave the bottle a few shakes.

"Did you know there's a Christmas tree farm in Hope Crossing?" Aunt Dee paused beside the counter.

Handing the bottle to Tyler, Audrey felt her eyes widen. "No, I did not." She cut a glance toward her aunt. "How come no one ever told me about this?"

Dee shrugged. "Guess it slipped my mind. From what I hear, it's quite an event. Cut your own tree, fresh garlands and wreaths."

Her excitement building, Audrey said, "Where is it? I need to visit this place."

"I'm glad to hear that—" Aunt Dee wagged a finger "—because I need a Christmas tree. If you'll recall, my pre-lit one died midway through Christmas Day last year."

Audrey gasped. "That's right. I'd forgotten all about that." And with tomorrow being Black Friday, they may well have missed out on the best pre-lit trees.

"Well, you're in good company. If it wasn't for this here movie we're watchin', I might not've remembered until we put the thing up." She waved a hand. "But it also reminded me about the tree farm. And since tomorrow is their opening day, I thought maybe the two of you—" she gestured from Audrey to Tyler and back "—could run over there in the mornin' and pick us up a nice one."

First she almost kissed Tyler, now he was being pushed into helping her again.

Audrey glared at her aunt. "What? You don't want to pick out your own tree?"

"Hon, folks'll be linin' up at the break of dawn. By the time I got over there, all the good trees would be gone. Besides, I've had the experience of cuttin' down a tree when I was a little girl, and my folks used to pick out one here at the ranch. Usually just a cedar, but I didn't know the difference." She shrugged. "Looked like a Christmas tree to me." Waving a hand, she continued.

"At any rate, I thought you'd probably leap at the opportunity. Except you're gonna need Tyler's muscles, not to mention his truck."

Audrey looked at Meredith as she joined them. "You should come with us."

"I can't. I have to be back in Houston by lunchtime."

"And Tessa and Dirk are taking the boys to Sea World in San Antonio," added Dee.

Audrey was starting to suspect a conspiracy.

"Besides, you're the Christmas queen," said Meredith.

"She sure is." Aunt Dee grinned. "I know you'll find us a humdinger of a tree."

Moving Willow to his shoulder, Tyler said, "Audrey, it's alright with me." His smile was rather childlike. "I've never been to a Christmas tree farm before." He lifted a shoulder. "Sounds kind of fun."

She hated being outnumbered. Though the glimmer in Tyler's eyes was winning her over. "In that case, what time should I expect you?"

"If they open at eight, do you think seven would be good?"

After a thumbs-up from Aunt Dee, Tyler took Willow back to the cabin, but not before Dee fixed a care package of food to send with him. Then Audrey grabbed her iPad and pulled up the Web site for the tree farm, pleasantly surprised at all they had to offer. Even a store. So by the time Tyler picked her up the next morning, her mind was awhirl with plenty of yuletide possibilities that helped take her mind off what happened yesterday.

The sun was barely peeking over the eastern horizon when she climbed into the cab of Tyler's truck, armed with two insulated tumblers full of coffee.

"I thought you might want this." She handed one to him before nestling hers in the cup holder and closing the passenger door. "It's nippy out there this morning."

"It sure is." He watched her buckle her seatbelt. "About yesterday…"

Her smile vanished as her heart twisted. She did not want to be reminded of how she'd embarrassed herself.

"I was out of line," he continued. "You were doing me a favor, offering to help me. And I read way too much into something that was merely a friendly gesture."

Wait. *He'd* read too much into it?

Blinking, she held up a hand. "Stop. It's alright. We both got wrapped up in a moment. That's all it was. I'm not offended or upset." And she'd prayed all night that he wasn't, either. "As far as I'm concerned, nothing has changed. We're friends. We enjoy each other's company. So let's go have some fun and find the best Christmas tree ever."

His smile returned. "Alright!"

Though the line of vehicles stretched down the road from the tree farm, once they opened the gate, things moved quickly. As Tyler parked, she glanced his way. "Did you bring the sling?"

"I did."

"In that case, since you'll probably be the one felling the tree, why don't you let me carry Willow?"

His grin grew bigger. "Felling a tree. Good thing I wore my lumberjack shirt." Gesturing to the buffalo check flannel, he peered out the windshield, taking in the multitude of lights and decorations, his expression reminding her of the night she'd surprised him with the Christmas tree. Making her, once again, wonder about his childhood.

With Tyler's help, she had Willow situated in short order, then with "Holly Jolly Christmas" carrying on the breeze, they followed the signs to the check-in point on the festively decorated porch of the red metal barn. Lights and decorations seemed to be everywhere they looked. They even had one of those old red Christmas tree trucks.

"This place is incredible." Tyler's wide gaze roamed the area. "I've never seen anything quite like it."

Audrey was doing her own share of gawking,

taking pictures and mentally making notes for ideas she could use at the ranch.

Once they'd checked in, they were presented with a measuring stick, a tree tag and a saw, before being directed to a flatbed trailer hauled by a tractor that would carry them into the seemingly endless maze of trees.

Tyler helped her onto the trailer before taking a seat beside her. A short time later, they were dropped off near a plot of Virginia pines and the search was on.

"What do you think?" He wove in and out of the trees, eyes sparkling as he encircled them, discounting those he deemed less than perfect. "About a seven-footer?"

"That sounds good."

He was a man on a mission, alright. But it was more than that. That same childish air she found more than a little endearing radiated from him. It also piqued her curiosity.

So, as they started down the next aisle, Tyler keeping pace beside her as they surveyed their options, she said, "Tell me what your Christmases were like when you were a child."

His smile faltered. And he looked everywhere but at her. "They were pretty low-key." He shrugged. "My mom didn't make a big deal about it."

While she sensed he was holding back, she decided to let it go. "I get it. I suppose my family is a bit of an exception. Myself, in particular. I can't seem to get enough. However, it is a lot of work." Nudging him with her elbow, she added, "As you can attest to."

His smile returned. "I don't mind." He stopped then, eyeing a nice specimen of tree. Moving closer, he circled it before checking the height. Glancing her way, he said, "This one looks close to perfect. What do you think?"

After an initial assessment, she also rounded the tree, nodding. "I think we have a winner."

She took multiple shots of the three of them in front of the tree, then more of him sawing the tree. Then they tagged it and awaited their ride back to the barn.

While the tree was shaken and bailed, they perused the various food offerings outside while enjoying some spiced cider, before visiting the shop inside the barn where she purchased some candles, and a lumberjack ornament she couldn't resist. It definitely belonged on Tyler's tree.

Yet despite Tyler's enjoyment of the day's events, there seemed to be an undercurrent of sadness ever since she'd brought up his childhood. And given that he'd never really talked about that part of his life, she could only wonder why.

Once the tree was loaded and secured in the bed of his truck, they started back to the ranch. Tyler was uncharacteristically quiet as they drove, making her wonder if her question about his childhood had stirred up unwanted memories.

Lord, whatever hurts Tyler is dealing with, I pray that You might grant him peace and loosen the strongholds that prevent him from living the life You've called him to.

As they neared the entrance to the ranch, Tyler said, "My dad left us on Christmas Day."

Jerking her head his way, she noticed the pulsating of his jaw, leaving her uncertain as to how or if she should respond.

"We never celebrated Christmas after that," he continued. "No tree. No decorations. No gifts. It was just another day, one my mom always volunteered to work because she got double time."

Tears blurred Audrey's vision. She couldn't fathom what that must have been like for Tyler and his sister. To be surrounded by kids at school who were eagerly anticipating the holiday, knowing it was nothing more than just another day for them. One they didn't even get to spend with their mother.

She sucked in a breath as they bumped over the cattle guard beneath the arched sign that now boasted evergreen garland and lights, well aware that Tyler wouldn't want her sympathy.

"And then I met you." Both hands on the wheel, he kept his eyes on the winding drive. "Little Miss Christmas." The corners of his mouth lifted as he darted a glance her way. "You showed me how wonderful Christmas could be. Even though our focus wasn't on Jesus, I experienced the joy of the season for the first time ever." His Adam's apple bobbed. "Then you were gone. So having a Christmas tree would've been like pouring salt on a wound. I had no reason to celebrate. Until I met Jesus." He swallowed hard. "Instead of a Christmas tree, I bought a manger scene. Nothing elaborate, just Jesus, Mary and Joseph. I set it up on a small table beneath a rugged wooden cross I made and hung on the wall. Because He's the greatest gift I could ever receive."

A tear spilled onto her cheek, followed by another. She swiped them away as more threatened. "Beauty for ashes."

He glanced her way. "I guess so."

"You must think all my planning and decorating foolish."

"Not at all. It brings people joy." He reached for her hand. "Including me."

Smiling, she squeezed it. "In that case, let's go spread some more joy."

Chapter Thirteen

Basking in the warm glow of lights from his Christmas tree Monday evening, Tyler held a freshly bathed Willow in his lap, phone pressed to his ear as the aroma of baby lotion hung in the air. "I mean it, Reid. This may have been one of the most incredible weekends of my life."

He, Audrey and Aunt Dee had gotten the Christmas tree set up Friday, going so far as to add lights, but since Dirk, Tessa and the boys didn't get back from San Antonio until late, they'd waited until Saturday evening to decorate it, much to the boys' chagrin. But Aunt Dee had insisted the entire family go over to the tent cabin area Saturday to prep things for Christmas Under the Stars.

The weather had been perfect for doing some general cleanup, as well as prepping for the bonfire. While the boys, Audrey and Tessa gathered smaller pieces of wood, Aunt Dee hauled in some downed tree limbs with her tractor, putting both Dirk and Tyler to work with the chainsaws. Then they returned to the area Sunday afternoon to add more lights and decorations, before plugging it all in and making sure everything worked properly.

"Are you serious?" Reid's incredulous tone was hard to miss. "You really told Audrey everything?"

"Yes, sir, I sure did." Tyler couldn't quite believe it, either. Not only had he made a fool of himself by trying to kiss Audrey, he'd followed it up by dumping his life story on her. The real story with all its warts. Things he'd never told anyone but Reid. Now Tyler was able to stand a little taller, knowing he had a clear conscience.

"And how do you feel about it?" Reid asked.

Tyler sighed as Willow grabbed hold of his finger. "Like a burden has been lifted. I never realized how I'd let all of those things I was so ashamed of weigh me down."

"You know they weren't yours to carry in the first place, Tyler. The blood of Jesus has set you free."

"Yeah, well, sometimes we know things in our heads, but find them hard to believe in our hearts."

"I can surely appreciate that. I don't suppose you've decided when you'll be coming back to Fort Worth, have you?"

Tyler winced. That was a topic he tried hard *not* to think about. Especially after this weekend. Strange how he'd come to Legacy Ranch to get

Audrey to sign a paper, hoping for closure, and now he couldn't help feeling as though a new beginning could be within his reach.

Working and living here these last several weeks had made him feel connected to not only the people, but the land they cherished. It was a feeling he'd never experienced before, nor could he explain it. All he knew was that he didn't want it to end.

Shifting in the chair, he adjusted Willow so she could see the tree better. "Christmas Under the Stars is Saturday evening, so next week at the earliest." Though he was starting to think it would be nice to stay through Christmas.

A text alert had him looking at the screen. And he couldn't help smiling when he saw Audrey's name.

Are you ready to call it a night, or may I join you for a few minutes?

"Hey, Reid, mind if I let you go? It looks like I'm about to have some company."

"No problem. Hang in there, brother. I'm proud of you."

Tyler's chest swelled. "Thank you, man."

After ending the call, he texted Audrey.

Come on down.

His heart pounded at the prospect. Looking at Willow, he said, "Audrey's coming to see us. What do you think about that?"

When her eyes finally met his, she smiled. Something that never failed to melt his heart. They'd come so far since being here. Because of Audrey and Aunt Dee, he felt competent caring for Willow. And the love he felt for her was unlike anything he'd ever felt before. Completely unconditional and pure. He would move mountains for his baby girl.

His baby girl?

The thought jolted him. But it was true. Willow would never remember Carrie. Only him. And even though he'd make sure she knew about her mother, he was the one who'd be there for every birthday and milestone. Who'd comfort her when she had a bad dream and cheer her on at soccer or whatever else she chose to do. They even shared the same last name, so everyone would assume she was his daughter.

Headlights glowed outside the window, announcing Audrey's arrival. She'd spent a good part of the day at cabin two, awaiting a couple of deliveries. Once the furniture arrived, Aunt Dee had joined her, eager to see her dream taking shape. Another day or so and they'd have it ready to show off.

Standing, he went to the door, opening it at the same time he flipped on the porch light. He couldn't help smiling as Audrey exited her vehicle. "To what do we owe this honor?"

Amid the cool evening air, she stepped onto the porch carrying her laptop and wearing yet another Christmas shirt over a pair of black joggers. Today's offering read *Jesus is the reason for the season.*

"We've been so busy, I keep forgetting to mention I've found some housing options I wanted to run past you."

The wind left his sails. "Wh-when did you find time to do that?"

With a shrug, she said, "Early in the morning, late at night." She nodded toward the cabin. "Let's go inside so I can show you."

He stepped out of the way, feeling as though reality had kicked him in the gut.

"Hello, sweet girl." Audrey smiled as she passed. "Are you enjoying your Christmas tree?"

Closing the door, he turned. "She sure is. She seems almost captivated by it."

"It's all the lights." Audrey set her laptop on the coffee table in front of the sofa and opened it before sitting down.

Still standing by the door, he said, "Can I get you anything? Decaf coffee? Water?" Anything else that might prolong him sitting and looking at the laptop.

She smiled his way. "No, I'm good." Patting the cushion beside her, she said, "Come join me."

Reluctantly, he crossed the short distance in his sock feet and eased beside her, inhaling the sunshine and wildflowers scent that was uniquely Audrey.

"So it appears that Johnson County—just south of Fort Worth—is one of the fastest-growing areas."

He watched as she pulled up several tabs. "I know. Our company has done several houses down there. A lot of the corporate builders are buying up ranches and farmland and chopping it into tiny lots."

"Yeah, I saw that." Frowning, she looked at him. "You own a construction company. So why not design and build your own house?"

"I thought about it. But by the time I decided on a design and the time it would take to build, we'd be looking at well over a year."

Her brow puckered as she twisted to face him. "I get that it takes time, but why the rush to find something now? I mean, you've got time. Willow won't be starting school for almost five years."

"I know, but our street has become so busy. I worry about her slipping outside without my knowledge and something happening. Once she's mobile, that is." Absently smoothing a hand over Willow's downy hair, he added, "And I guess I want her to have that sense of home that I never had. Carrie and I were bounced from one apartment to the next, changing schools more often than not." He looked at Audrey. "One year, I attended three different schools."

Her expression softened. "Tyler, it's not the structure that makes a home, it's the people. You love Willow. And love is what she needs most of all. No matter where you live." Facing the computer once again, she added, "Though a busy street and an active toddler are not the best combination."

Running a finger over the touchpad, she said, "I did come across a couple of homes that might be good options. This one is new construction."

It was a good-looking home. Brick and stone. Single story with an open kitchen, three bedrooms, two and a half baths, even a bonus room. Yet as she walked him through it on the screen, he couldn't help thinking about the one thing that was missing from the equation.

Her.

Audrey lay on her stomach atop the living room rug at the ranch house a little before nine Wednesday morning, camera at the ready. "Come on, Willow. You can do it. Look at me."

Lying on her own tummy, backdropped by the lit Christmas tree near the window, Willow splayed her tiny fingers, her head bobbing as she attempted to comply.

"Let's show Tyler how strong you are. That all these weeks of tummy time are finally paying off."

When the baby lowered her head, Audrey stuck her tongue between her lips and blew.

Then, as if she had a sudden burst of energy, Willow lifted her little head—and she was smiling!

Audrey snapped several shots before Willow's strength finally gave out. "Good job, Willow." Moving to her knees, Audrey set the phone aside before lifting the child into her arms. "What a big, strong girl you are." She bent Willow's arm at the elbow. "Just look at those muscles. I think that deserves a treat. What do you say? A bottle for you, coffee for me. With some peppermint creamer. For me, that is. You're not ready for that yet."

Standing, she went into the kitchen and tucked Willow into her bouncy seat atop the table before preparing a bottle and filling her holiday mug with coffee and a splash of creamer. But when Willow seemed content batting at the toys on her seat, Audrey put the bottle in the refrigerator and sat down at the table.

She opened her phone, selected one of the photos she'd just taken and typed out a text to Tyler.

Look what our girl can do.

She was about to hit Send, when she realized what she'd typed. *Our* girl. She and Tyler weren't an *our*. Nor did Willow belong to her in any way, shape or form. But that hadn't stopped Audrey from loving her. No doubt about it, saying goodbye was going to be tough. Her entire routine would change without Willow around.

But then, this had been a good test for her. Given her a glimpse of what her life would be like when she had her own child. Not to mention built her confidence, proving that she would be able to handle being a single mother. Besides, between the holidays and all the work that lay ahead on the barn, she'd have plenty to keep her busy once Willow was gone. Though without Tyler here to run all her plans by and let her know what would and would not work, she'd have to learn to trust her own instincts.

She sighed. He was right. They did make a good team.

After changing her text to Look what Willow can do, she hit Send and took a sip of her drink.

Seconds later, he texted back.

She's growing so fast.

No doubt about that. Scrolling through her photos, Audrey couldn't help noticing how many she'd taken of Willow over the eight weeks she and Tyler had been here at the ranch. Audrey hadn't realized how much the child had grown and changed during that time. She'd lost that newborn look and transformed into a bright-eyed baby girl. One who definitely favored Tyler.

Speaking of change, Tyler was not the same man she'd walked out on four years ago. Nor was she the same insecure woman. And she couldn't help thinking that they knew each other better now than they had when they were married.

Pausing on an image of the three of them at the Christmas tree farm, one question played through her mind. What if?

What if she and Tyler had communicated better? What if they'd been Christians? What if God was granting them a second chance?

She jolted at that last notion. "No. It would never work." Tyler's life was in Fort Worth. Hers was here at Legacy Ranch. It wasn't like she was going to abandon Aunt Dee.

Scrolling once again, she felt a smile tugging at the corners of her mouth as an idea formed. She needed to have all these images made into prints so she could assemble a photo album for Tyler. Something he could add to as Willow grew. Physical photo albums seemed like a rarity in today's device-driven world, but they were something that could be cherished.

Maybe she'd give it to him for Christmas. Then she remembered he'd be gone by then. Ignoring the unwanted discomfort in the vicinity of her heart, she decided to do it anyway and give it to him before he left. Something to commemorate Willow's first Christmas.

Willow began to fuss.

Abandoning her phone, Audrey stood and retrieved the bottle from the refrigerator. "Did you finally work up an appetite?" After putting the bottle into the warmer, she picked up the frowning child. "It'll be ready in just a minute."

A short time later, Audrey carried her into the living room and settled into one of the chairs so she and Willow could enjoy the Christmas tree. Just as she got situated, her phone dinged with a text from Tyler.

Willow's 4m checkup is today! Completely slipped my mind.

Audrey jolted. She'd forgotten, too. Must be all the activity.

She bounced a thumb over the screen.

No problem. I can take her. What time?

Dots wobbled across the screen as he typed.

11. Consent forms will need my sig.

Her thumb hovered over the screen as she worried her bottom lip. Should she offer to go with him? With all the silly thoughts that had been tumbling through her head, that might not be such a good idea.

Ignoring the bubbles on the screen, she started typing as his next message popped up.

Will you come too?

Her heart gave an excited leap. Before she could second-guess herself, she deleted what she'd been typing and sent a thumbs-up. It was just a doctor's appointment. Not some intimate rendezvous.

Once Willow finished her bottle, Audrey changed her. She was about to run upstairs when she heard a vehicle outside. Recognizing Tyler's truck, she waited for him. At the sound of his boots coming up the steps, she opened the door.

"I need to run upstairs for a second." She passed Willow off to him. "Go ahead and put her in her seat and I'll be right back."

"You got it."

Still in her sock feet, she hurried up the stairs to her room. Then she shoved her feet into a pair of booties with a chunky heel and pulled her hair into a ponytail before hurrying back downstairs.

Tyler stood beside the door, holding Willow's seat with her in it. "Slow down. We've got plenty of—"

Suddenly, Audrey's right foot buckled, just before it slid out from beneath her. Fighting to regain her balance, she stumbled down the handful of steps that remained, falling to her knees when she reached the bottom.

"Audrey, are you alright?" Tyler knelt beside her.

Giving herself a stern shake, she said, "I think so."

He helped her to her feet. "You're sure? Maybe you should stay here."

Regaining her wits, she hauled in a deep breath. "No, I'm fine. Let's go."

She stepped onto the porch, the bright sunshine warming her face as she carefully descended the steps, trying to ignore the throbbing in her ankle. If it was still bothering her when she got home, she'd put some ice on it.

As they pulled away from the ranch, she noticed Tyler kept looking her way.

"I said I'm fine."

"Yeah, well, I said the same thing when I smacked my head and you and Aunt Dee kept me down the rest of the day."

Looking his way, she said, "Last time I checked, my brain isn't in my ankle." His frown had her adding, "I appreciate your concern, though."

Time to change the subject. "How are things coming on the other three tent cabins?"

"Good." One hand on the steering wheel, he kept his focus on the road ahead. "The interior work should be finished by Friday, maybe early next week. Then we'll turn things over to you so you can work your wonders on the insides."

That made her smile, despite the throbbing in her foot. With Dirk having to split his time between there and the barn while the concrete people worked the last two days setting their forms, she'd been a little concerned. Thankfully, the new foundation was supposed to be poured tomorrow morning, and then things could get back to normal.

Arriving at the urgent care, Tyler parked before retrieving Willow while Audrey eased herself from the truck cab, hoping not to jolt her foot. Yet while she was successful, the act of walking normally was nothing less than torture.

"How's the foot?" Tyler opened the door to the medical office.

"Fine." Alright, maybe not exactly fine. She sure was looking forward to that ice pack.

While Tyler checked Willow in at the reception desk, Audrey sat in one of the padded chairs in the Texas-themed waiting room.

When Tyler joined her, he unhooked Willow and lifted her into his arms. "You ready to see how big you've gotten?"

Audrey loved it when he talked to Willow, using that childlike voice that was reserved only for her.

Perched on his lap, the infant looked Audrey's

way, watching her as if she suspected something wasn't quite right.

No, that was just Audrey's imagination. Nonetheless, she focused on the Christmas tree with multicolor lights, tucked beside the reception desk.

"Willow?" a female voice called out.

Tyler stood, Willow in one arm, the carrier in his other hand.

Meanwhile, Audrey grabbed the backpack and sucked in a breath as she pushed to her feet, willing herself to ignore the pain. By the time they reached the small examination room, Audrey all but crumpled into the chair. She needed some over-the-counter pain reliever. Then she realized she'd forgotten her purse.

Biting back a groan, she prayed. *Lord God, please, heal my ankle. Let it be nothing more than a bruise.*

When the nurse practitioner came in, Audrey remained seated, watching as the woman close to her own age checked Willow over and took some measurements. But when it came time for Willow's immunizations, Audrey had to look away. Even then, Willow's pathetic cries had Audrey on the verge of tears herself.

"She's a healthy little girl." The nurse smiled as Tyler held Willow close, looking as though he might never let her go. "You can use a cool compress on the injection site, or if it really bothers her, you're welcome to give her some infant over-the-counter pain reliever."

He nodded then. "Thank you."

After dressing Willow and buckling her into her seat, he looked Audrey's way. "I'm ready when you are."

"Okay." By sheer will, she pushed to her feet—make that foot. "I'm right behind you." Yet by the time she stepped into the corridor, she could feel sweat forming on her brow.

You can do this, Audrey. There's ice and pain reliever at home.

Yet before she even made it to the reception area, her foot gave out and she collapsed.

"Help!" she heard Tyler call out.

The next thing Audrey knew, she was in an examination room, filling out multiple forms before the same nurse practitioner came in.

After listening to Audrey's story and examining her now bootless—not to mention swollen—right foot and doing an X-ray, the woman said, "I don't see any sign of a fracture. However, sprains can be just as—if not more—painful. So over-the-counter pain reliever, as needed. Also I want you to stay off it and keep it elevated as much as possible."

"I can't do that. We're preparing for a big holiday event Saturday."

"You can, and you will." Tyler scowled at her.

The nurse's gaze darted between them. "This wouldn't happen to be at Legacy Ranch, would it?"

"Yes, it is."

"Oh." The other woman smiled. "My family and I are planning to attend."

That made Audrey smile. "That's great. We're looking forward to a wonderful evening."

Her gaze darting from Tyler to Audrey, the nurse lowered her voice. "Your ankle should feel better in a couple of days. In the meantime, I suggest executing the art of delegation."

Not exactly her forte. But between Tyler and Aunt Dee, she doubted she'd have a choice.

Chapter Fourteen

By the time the sun set Saturday evening, dozens of vehicles were parked in the grassy area a sufficient distance away from the bonfire as Christmas Under the Stars got underway. The weather couldn't have been more perfect. Cool enough for those Christmas sweaters, yet warm enough not to have to cover them up with jackets or coats.

Amid the abundance of Christmas lights they'd put up and holiday tunes carrying through the air via Bluetooth speakers, Audrey and Meredith helped Aunt Dee at the check-in table before sending guests on to Tessa, Dirk and her boys, who instructed them where to leave their appetizers, sides and desserts, as well as pointing out the snowy evergreen background Tessa had painted for a photo booth and some carnival-style games for the kids—Pin the Nose on Rudolph, the Candy Cane Tree (a takeoff on the traditional lollipop game) and Reindeer Ring Toss.

"Be sure to put your name and contact information on one of these tickets." Sitting at a table, wearing a shimmering red sweater over dark wash jeans and dress boots that afforded her a much more feminine look than her usual attire, Aunt Dee looked up at the young mother. "We're givin' away a stay at one of these beautiful cabins." Gesturing to the tent cabins behind them, she added, "Cabin number two is open if you'd like to have a look-see."

The other woman and her husband grinned.

"We'll definitely check it out," said the husband.

"Audrey." With Willow in the sling, Tyler leaned a folding chair against the table, before opening a second and positioning it beside her. "You need to get off that ankle."

"It's doing fine. I wrapped it and purposely wore these low-heeled riding boots."

Still holding on to the back of the chair, he said, "Aunt Dee is sitting down, so there's no reason you can't, too. Please?"

The concern in his eyes had warm fuzzies flitting through her. Tyler had been nothing less than attentive since her mishap Wednesday. Even after the pain and swelling had subsided yesterday morning, he'd been at her beck and call, making sure she didn't do any more than necessary. And while she wasn't particularly fond of having her movements restricted, his devotion stirred up countless emotions, most of which exceeded the boundaries of friendship.

"Thank you." Her cheeks heating, she sat down.

"Meredith, I brought a chair for you, too."

"Oh, thank you, Tyler."

Flanking their aunt, they watched as an older gentleman stepped forward. His brown hair had only a smidge of gray at the temples, and there was a definite sparkle in his eyes. He was also *very* handsome.

"Hello, D'Lynn."

His greeting had her aunt's movements stilling before she slowly lifted her gaze to his. "M-Mark."

Never looking away from Dee, he smiled. "You're as lovely as ever."

"Wh-what are you doin' here?" The woman who was never at a loss for words had yet to look away.

Audrey caught Meredith's attention on the other side of Dee, though her sister simply shrugged.

"I recently moved back to the area," he said. "I'm living out at our family property."

Unable to stay quiet any longer, Audrey held out her hand. "Welcome to Legacy Ranch. I'm Audrey, D'Lynn's niece."

Nodding, he took hold of her hand. "Mark Walters." He darted a glance toward her aunt before returning his attention to Audrey. "I'm an old friend of D'Lynn's. Not that she's old, mind you."

"No, she's most definitely not old." Audrey smiled.

On her feet now, Meredith said, "She runs circles around all of us." Then she offered her hand. "Meredith Hunt."

"Good to make your acquaintance, ladies."

Clearing her throat, Aunt Dee said, "Here's your raffle ticket. Though a stay at one of these here tent cabins—" she poked a half-hearted thumb that way "—might mean lowerin' your standards."

What? Why would her aunt talk to a guest like that?

Despite Aunt Dee's rudeness, he eyed the cabins that had been decked out with lights for the holiday season. "Very intriguing."

"Cabin two is open, if you'd like to take a look." Audrey smiled.

"I believe I'll do just that." He looked from Audrey to Meredith. "Lovely to meet you, ladies." Then, smiling at her aunt, he said, "I hope we have an opportunity to talk later."

Dee watched after him as he walked away. "Don't count on it."

"Aunt Dee!" Audrey returned to her chair. "What has gotten into you?"

Still staring after him, she said, "Let's just say time does *not* heal all wounds."

"Can I have your attention please?" Pastor

Green used a microphone they'd borrowed from the church.

As the crowd filled with infants, elderly and people of every age in between quieted, he continued. "We're just about ready to eat, but before I bless the food, I want to extend a hearty thank you to Miss D'Lynn Hunt and her family for sharing their beautiful ranch with us as we gather to celebrate the greatest gift ever, our Lord and Savior, Jesus Christ."

Raucous applause and whistles ensued.

Once things quieted, he continued. "We've got plenty of tables and chairs over here, so y'all enjoy supper with some friends, then we've got some entertainment courtesy of our youth and children's groups. Won't you bow your heads, please."

The next two hours were filled with fun, food and the antics of some pretty talented teens who had everyone laughing. The children's group—which included her nephews, Grayson and Bryce—led the entire crowd in some Christmas carols. Then Pastor closed things out with a brief message before leading everyone in a chorus of "Silent Night." And as Audrey looked up at the vast expanse of starry sky, she couldn't help but contemplate that first Christmas so long ago.

After announcing the winners of the drawing—a young couple with two small children—folks in attendance helped break down and load the tables and chairs into Dirk's trailer so he could take them back to the church in the morning. Then, as the fire dwindled and all the guests departed, the games, photo booth, dishes and other incidentals were tucked in the back of Aunt Dee's truck as the family prepared to head back to the house.

Still basking in the joy of the evening, Audrey said, "Y'all go on. I still need to gather the speakers and unplug some lights."

"Someone'll need to stay to give you a ride back." Aunt Dee's gaze darted to Tyler. He still had Willow in the sling, though Audrey didn't know if she was awake or asleep. Likely the latter, since it was nearing nine o'clock.

"I don't mind," he said.

"In that case, why don't you let me take Little Miss?" Her aunt approached. "The girls and I can give her a bath, that way she'll be ready for bed when you pick her up."

Removing the baby from the sling, he said, "I appreciate that. Thank you. Let me get her carrier out of the truck."

Soon, Audrey watched the rest of her family drive away, taillights glowing in the darkness. "This was amazing." She turned her attention to Tyler. "I can't thank you enough for everything you did to help make this happen. I couldn't have done it without you."

"First of all, yes, you could have. Second, it

was my pleasure. It was fun to see everything come together. Now we just need to finish out the rest of the tent cabins and you'll be ready to start hosting guests."

She felt her smile grow. "I can't wait. Now, let's get those lights unplugged."

The night air was still as, little by little, the area around them grew darker. While she continued to bask in the joy this night had brought, Tyler turned off the final porch light at cabin two, leaving only the stars above to illuminate their path.

Looking up, she found herself filled with a sense of awe at the tapestry of God's handiwork. When she sensed Tyler approaching, she said, "You don't see stars like this in the city."

"No, you sure don't." He stepped in front of her then. "I'm curious. Who was that guy—Mark, I think he said was his name—that seemed to rub Aunt Dee the wrong way?"

Audrey slowly shook her head. "I have no idea. All I know is that I've never seen her behave with such disdain. However, I do intend to do a little prodding and see what I can find out, so I'll keep you posted."

They fell silent then, and when his fingers touched hers, she greedily entwined them.

"I cannot tell you how much I've enjoyed spending these last couple of months with you and your family." He inched closer. "Though I think getting reacquainted with you has been my favorite part."

"Mine, too." As she peered into his eyes, an unexpected sensation sifted through her. A yearning for something more than just Tyler's friendship. And to her surprise, she welcomed it. "I like the man you've become, Tyler."

"I'm rather fond of you, too." His gaze was unwavering. And ever so slightly, his face drew closer to hers.

Then she pushed up on her toes, the twinge in her right foot barely noticeable as her lips met his. She'd always loved his kisses, but this—*this*—was even better than she recalled.

Releasing her hand, he wound his arms around her waist and pulled her close. He smelled of smoke and outdoors, this rugged man with a tender heart—a heart he'd finally given her access to. And despite her own iron-fisted grip, she was afraid she'd let go of hers, too.

At the log cabin early Sunday morning, Tyler lay in his bed, staring into the rafters as images of last night played through his mind like a highlights reel. Though while he mentally fast-forwarded through many of them, there was one that lingered.

The moment his lips touched Audrey's, he'd felt as though all was right with his world. As if the shattered pieces of the last four years had been put back in place, held together by the glue of grace and forgiveness. And for the first time in—well, maybe ever—he had hope.

Now he just had to figure out how to proceed going forward. In a few short weeks, he'd be returning to Fort Worth. Meanwhile, Audrey would be here, overseeing guest accommodations, as well as the soon-to-be venue.

He supposed they'd need to talk about their future—at least, he assumed there was one—and where they went from here. Because the thought of losing Audrey again was too much to bear. He loved her. And while he supposed he'd always loved her, this was different. Deeper. Stronger. They'd connected on more than just a superficial level. They'd revealed their hearts to one another. Their scars and warts. Yet from that, something new and beautiful had emerged.

Willow's cooing drifted to the loft, and he couldn't help smiling. His little girl deserved a mama. And he couldn't think of anyone more fit for that role than Audrey.

Tossing the covers aside, he flipped on the bedside lamp before making his way down the stairs in basketball shorts and a T-shirt, a smile on his face at the anticipation of seeing Audrey at church. He'd have to text her and see if she'd like to ride together.

While it was still dark outside, the dim light from the loft was enough for him to see his sweet baby girl as he approached. She'd managed to free her arms from her swaddling and excitedly batted them about. She'd been asleep when he picked her up last night, not long after that fortuitous kiss, and had remained that way until somewhere around three this morning. All that fresh air must've worn her out.

"Good morning, Willow."

Her arms moved faster, her tiny mouth starting to pout.

"Hey now." Picking her up, he held her close. "What's with the pouty face? I'm right here."

She gave a little coo and smiled at him.

After turning on the Christmas tree lights, he changed her diaper and readied her bottle before settling into the chair near the fireplace. Then, while Willow chugged her breakfast, he checked the news and weather on his phone as the sun came up.

With Willow satisfied, Tyler placed her in the bouncy seat before texting Audrey about riding together. And was pleased with her prompt response in the affirmative.

Once he was properly groomed, he went upstairs to don a pair of dark-wash jeans and a blue-and-white oxford before grabbing a pair of socks and returning to the main level for his boots. Now he just had to determine what Willow was going to wear.

He was rummaging through a stack of her

clothing that he kept in one of the storage cubbies along the wall outside the bathroom when his phone began vibrating. Pulling it from the pocket of his jeans, he looked at the screen, perplexed when he saw Reid's wife's name staring back at him.

Tapping the speaker icon, he said, "Shannon? How are you?"

"Not too good, Tyler." Her voice quivered. "Um." She sniffed. "I'm at the hospital with Reid. It's his heart."

Abandoning his search, he shuffled to the couch and dropped onto the cushion. "Is...is he okay?"

"They're prepping him for surgery."

Tyler's heart raced as the implications of her statement began to register. Reid was the greatest man Tyler had ever known. Part father figure, part friend and mentor, Reid had helped guide him out of one of the darkest periods of Tyler's life, and God knew he'd had plenty of those. Reid had shown him the way to a new life in Christ.

What if Reid died?

"Which hospital?" Making a mental note of her response, he said, "I'll be there as quick as I can."

Ending the call, he dragged a hand through his hair as sorrow crouched around him.

No, he wouldn't go there. His friend was still with them. And Tyler needed to pray it would remain that way.

He dropped to his knees and bent God's ear, pleading his friend's case. When he'd finished, he began gathering up everything that belonged to him and Willow. Thankfully, Willow had fallen back to sleep.

The morning air was cold when he stepped outside with a fistful of hanging clothes, so after slipping them over the hook in the back seat, he moved to the driver's seat to crank the engine and turned on the heater. He made several more trips until the only things left that belonged to him were the Christmas decorations.

I couldn't bear the thought of you not having a Christmas tree.

That night had marked a turning point in his and Audrey's relationship. On his end anyway. Though he'd never stopped loving her, that night she'd recaptured his heart anew. Now he was the one who had to walk away—without that tree. Between his tools and all of his and Willow's things, his truck was packed to the gills.

Maybe Audrey would want to go with you.

He'd toss out everything he owned to make room for her.

Should he ask her to go? If what happened last night was any indication, she'd want to be there to support him, just as he would for her if things were reversed.

After giving the log cabin a final once-over, he loaded Willow into her carrier, then grabbed it and her bouncy seat and started toward the door. When he'd first arrived at Legacy Ranch, he'd been a bumbling soul, trying to do right by Willow and failing miserably. And Audrey despised him. Now they were on the cusp of a second chance. One he wasn't about to let pass him by.

When he pulled up to the ranch house minutes later, he knew what he wanted. He wanted Audrey. Always and forever. More than that, he wanted to be the kind of husband she deserved. One who put her desires above his own. He wanted to be that man.

He retrieved Willow from the back seat, hurried up the walk and the steps, then knocked on the door.

A split second later, Aunt Dee swung it open. "Mornin', Tyler." She motioned him inside.

Moving past her, he said, "I need to talk to Audrey."

"Everthin' alright?" Dee's brow puckered in concern.

"Not exactly."

"Tyler?"

Lifting his gaze, he saw Audrey coming down the steps, all ready for church, save for the shoes dangling from her fingers. "I need to talk to you."

Confusion pleated her brow when she reached him. "Sure." She smoothed her free hand over his arm. "What's going on?"

"Reid's wife called. He's in the hospital. It's his heart."

"Oh, no." Her chestnut eyes grew wide as she took Willow's carrier from him and set it on the floor.

He started to pace, jabbing his fingers through his hair. "I need to go back to Fort Worth." And he wanted her to come with him. But how should he tell her that?

"Of course. He's your friend." She slipped her hand in the crook of his elbow.

Stopping, he simply stared down at her. She was everything he'd ever wanted.

Continuing to watch him, she said, "D-do you think you'll be back before Christmas?"

He shook his head. "I don't know. I have no idea what shape Reid is in. Someone has to be there to run the company."

He took her hands in his, meeting her gaze. "Come with me."

Her mouth fell open, her eyes widening. "What?"

"Come with me. I love you, Audrey. We can get married again. You've seen how good we can be together. We'll go to the Justice of the Peace. And you can pick out the house of your dreams. Just say you'll come with me."

Her countenance fell along with her shoulders. Slowly, she shook her head, pulling away from him. "I—I can't do that, Tyler. My life is here, at Legacy Ranch."

"What about last night? Everything was so perfect."

Taking a step back, she hugged herself. "We just got caught up in the moment."

It was then he realized how foolish he must sound. Begging had never been his style. "No, Audrey. I was not caught up in a moment. I was caught up in you. I love you." With that, he pressed a kiss to her cheek, picked up Willow's carrier and started toward the door where a sad-eyed Aunt Dee waited.

She reached for him, and he hugged her back. "I love you, Tyler."

He nodded, believing it was true. But without Audrey, he didn't belong here.

"Goodbye, Aunt Dee."

As he walked through the door and down the steps, a stout north wind sent a shiver down his spine. It was going to be a long ride home.

Chapter Fifteen

He hadn't taken the Christmas decorations. And Audrey wasn't sure if she wanted to cry or punch something.

With her hands full, she kicked the door from the carriage porch closed Tuesday afternoon before dropping the bag of towels and linens on the floor of the laundry room. Today was the first time she'd been able to bring herself to go down to the log cabin since Tyler and Willow left on Sunday. And seeing all the decorations—the tree, the stockings—right where she'd put them felt like a gut punch. They were a gift. She'd told him that. Yet he left them behind.

Kicking off her sneakers, she continued into the kitchen. In an effort to avoid the log cabin, she'd kept herself busy at the tent cabins since Tyler's abrupt departure, assembling and placing furniture, preparing the unique glamping units for guests. She still had a ways to go, but at least it had given her something else to focus on.

At the white top mount refrigerator, she threw open the door long enough to grab a mini Dr Pepper before tossing it closed. Tyler and Willow had been gone two and a half days, yet their scents still lingered in the cabin. Stripping the beds, she'd caught a whiff of Willow's baby lotion tinged with a hint of spit-up, not to mention Tyler's musky scent laced with smoke from Saturday night's bonfire. Any other time, the aromas might have had her swooning. Today, they annoyed her.

After chugging half the can, she heaved a sigh. She missed them.

"What's all the racket?"

Audrey jerked as her aunt entered from the hall.

"I could hear you grumblin' all the way in my bathroom while I was washin' up."

"Sorry, I thought I was alone."

Her aunt strolled toward her. "Tessa and the boys are here, too. Must be somethin' on your mind if you hadn't picked up on all that." She cocked her head. "Wouldn't have anything to do with Tyler, would it?"

Briefly closing her eyes, Audrey said, "I'd rather not talk about him, if you don't mind."

"Hey, you're back." Tessa's focus was on Audrey as she strolled into the kitchen. "Where have you been?"

"I had to go to the log cabin to gather laundry." Suddenly deciding her misery needed company, she perched a fist on her hip. "You aren't going to believe this. The Christmas tree and decorations I bought for Tyler? He left them." Even the lumberjack ornament.

Tessa and her aunt shared a look.

"Well—" Dee turned her way "—he did have to leave rather suddenly. He probably just overlooked them."

"Or he didn't have room in his truck," Tessa added. "Between his tools and everything else." She shrugged.

Cocking her head, Dee said, "He did ask you to go with him, though."

"More like demanded. As if I could just drop everything and run off with him." She shook her head.

"Why not?" Aunt Dee's blue eyes were fixed on Audrey. "That's what people do when they care about someone. And I suspect you care a lot more about Tyler than you're willin' to let on."

"He *told* me we could get married. At the JOP, no less." She rolled her eyes. "Like that's every woman's dream." Realizing what she'd said, she added, "I never even told him I loved him. He just assumed."

"Well, don't you?" Aunt Dee glared at her. "I mean, if you don't love him, then why are you so upset?"

"Good question." Tessa looked from their aunt to Audrey. "I could understand feeling bad that you'd hurt his feelings," she said, "but where's all this anger coming from?"

Audrey held up a hand. "I don't want to talk about it anymore." Looking at her aunt, she added, "Though there is something I think Tessa and I would both like to know."

"What's that?"

"What's the story with Mark Walters? I mean, talk about out of character. I've never seen you treat anyone that way."

"Yeah." Perching a hand on her hip, Tessa looked at Dee. "Did he treat you badly or something?"

Their aunt went rigid. "He's just someone I used to know."

"When?" asked Audrey.

Moving to the table, Aunt Dee slid into a chair. "We went to school together."

"Was he the class bully or something?" Audrey followed her, and so did Tessa. "Because I've never seen you so intimidated."

"I was *not* intimidated." Dee hiked her chin a notch. "There are just certain people I don't care to engage with, and he's one of them."

"How come?" Arms on the table, Audrey watched her aunt's face as she seemingly wrestled with something. "What did he do to you?"

Lips pursed, their aunt remained silent.

"Oh, no. You're not getting off that easily," said Audrey. "Especially after the way you've stuck your nose into both my and Tessa's love lives."

"Who said Mark Walters had anything to do with love?"

Audrey felt a smirk blossom. "Not me. But it looks like you just did."

Their aunt heaved a sigh. "Alright. He and I went steady back in high school. His family expected him to go to college and law school at one of those Ivy Leagues. He asked me to go with him, but I told him I wasn't leavin' the ranch. So, he went off without me and never came back."

Tessa leaned closer. "Did *he* ever marry?"

Dee nodded. "Had a couple of kids."

"Is he the reason you never married?"

Looking at Audrey as though she'd lost her mind, she said, "As if I'd let any man have that much power over me." She shook her head. "No, I just didn't like the feel of a broken heart, and determined I never wanted to go through that again. But what I hadn't expected was that all these decades later I'd still be askin' myself what if."

"I know just what you mean," said Tessa. "I'll always wonder, if I hadn't let Nick walk out the door that night, would my boys still have their father?"

Aunt Dee placed a hand atop Audrey's. "Sweet

thing, I know you're afraid of gettin' hurt again. But you and Tyler are different people now. And it's obvious that he's still head-over-heels in love with you. If you feel even an ounce of what I suspect you feel for him, don't spend the rest of your life wonderin' what if."

Audrey attempted to blink back her tears. "But what about the ranch? The cabins and venue."

"Audrey, you have embraced my plans for the ranch since the day I told you girls what I wanted to do. You sacrificed your life in Houston to come here and help me start bringing them to life. But you don't have to be here to do that. You do most everything online anyway." Squeezing Audrey's hand, she continued, "You love Tyler. And he loves you. I believe God brought you two back together for a reason."

Grabbing a napkin from the holder on the table, Audrey blotted her cheeks. "I'm afraid."

"Of what?"

"Failing again."

Dee cupped Audrey's chin. "The Bible says, 'There is no fear in love.'"

I was not caught up in a moment. I was caught up in you. I love you.

Despite Tyler's initial, frantic pleas, his parting words had been resolute. Genuine.

And the sudden awareness of that had her feeling all kinds of flustered. "I guess the good thing is, I know where to find Tyler." A nervous laugh bubbled out as she recalled her plans to make a photo album for him and Willow. "But before I can go, I have a few things I need to complete here."

Dee hiked a brow. "Such as?"

"The tent cabins and a Christmas gift." As she stood, Tessa caught her attention.

"I have one request."

Audrey looked at her sister, barely able to contain her excitement. "What's that?"

"If you do get married again, can we please be there to witness it?"

Audrey's cheeks heated at the notion. "I wouldn't have it any other way."

Tyler had gone directly to the hospital when he returned to Fort Worth Sunday and was relieved to learn that Reid was going to be fine. Turned out he had multiple blockages in his heart, requiring stents. Thankfully, Shannon's insistence he go to the emergency room had been the right move, and by the next day, Reid was feeling like a new man.

Still, it had left Tyler with a fair amount of regret. Taking off the way he had, staying away for months, leaving Reid to run the company solo. Alright, so they'd spoken often and gone over projects regularly. Still, Tyler couldn't help wondering if the added stress had brought on his friend's *episode*, as Reid called it.

Despite having Willow with him twenty-four-seven, Tyler went to the office every day. He'd worry about daycare when he had more time. Besides, the busier he stayed, the less time he had to dwell on Audrey.

Now, as he pulled up to Reid's two-story brick-and-stone home outlined with clear C5 Christmas lights late Wednesday afternoon, Tyler was looking forward to seeing his friend and mentor face-to-face. Because of Willow, he'd purposely stayed away, but since Shannon had not only offered, but practically begged for an opportunity to spend time with the baby, Tyler agreed.

After turning off the engine, he stepped out of his truck, lifting the collar of his heavy jacket. Winter had decided to pay an early visit to North Texas. Thankfully, it wasn't accompanied by any precipitation.

After adjusting the blanket over Willow, he removed her carrier from its base and made a hasty break for the house, nudging the truck door closed in the process.

The north wind nipped at his nose as he approached the entrance adorned with pine boughs and red ribbon, making him glad when the iron and glass door opened before he got there. A smiling Shannon waited on the other side, affording him a quick escape from the near-freezing temperatures.

"Look what the cat dragged in." Inside the

well-appointed home that smelled like cinnamon and cloves, a smiling Reid ambled across the festive foyer's wood flooring, wearing a pullover sweater and jeans.

Eyeing his friend, Tyler set the carrier on the floor as Shannon closed the door.

"Good to see you, brother." Beside him now, Reid wrapped Tyler in a manly hug.

"Good to see me?" With a final pat on the back, Tyler released the man with short black hair and the beginning of a beard that sported more gray than black. "I'm *thrilled* to see you. You scared me half to death."

"You're not the only one." Coming alongside her husband, Shannon looped her sweater-covered arm through his and stared up at the man.

Seeing the love Reid and Shannon shared had Tyler's heart feeling as though it was in a vise. He'd dared to dream that he and Audrey could have another chance at that kind of love. Obviously, he'd misread things.

Reid looked from his bride to Tyler. "Good news for both of you. God's not finished with me yet."

Eyeing the carrier, Shannon knelt and reached for Willow's blanket. "Where's that sweet baby girl?" She withdrew the covering. "There she is."

Bundled in a pink snowsuit, Willow took in her surroundings, her eyes wide. Then she looked at Shannon and smiled.

Pressing a hand to her chest, the woman sighed. "She is just precious, Tyler." She glanced up at him. "She's got your eyes."

"So I've been told."

As she proceeded to unbuckle Willow, Shannon said, "If you two want to retreat to Reid's study, Willow and I will be just fine."

Remembering the backpack over his shoulder, Tyler slid it from his arm and eased it to the floor. "It's freshly stocked, in case you need anything."

"Can I get you something to drink?" Reid eyed him. "Coffee?"

"Only if it's already made. I don't want either of you to go to any trouble."

"You don't know my wife very well, do you?" His mentor set a hand on Tyler's back as they started toward the kitchen. "Come on."

When they finally settled into Reid's study that also boasted a pool table and wall-mounted flat-screen—Reid on one side of the wooden executive desk while Tyler took the cushioned chair opposite—Tyler listened while Reid gave him more details about his ordeal, while the older man wanted to know everything that had transpired at Legacy Ranch.

After telling his mentor about his hasty departure, Reid sent him an incredulous look. "You told her you could get married again? At the Justice of the Peace?" He shook his head. "Son, have you not learned anything? You can't just tell a woman you love her, you've got to show her. But the Justice of the Peace? I oughta thump you upside the head for that one. What were you thinking?"

With his right ankle perched atop his left knee, Tyler slouched. "I don't know. I was worried about you and in a hurry to get back." Looking away, he sighed. "But having to leave her was killing me."

"It certainly robbed you of a few brain cells."

Dropping his foot to the carpet, he straightened. "Yeah, well, if you don't calm down, Shannon's going to kick me out."

Reid waved him off. "Ah, they got those blockages taken care of. I'm fine. You, on the other hand, look miserable."

"I am." He dragged a hand through his hair. "I still love Audrey. And I thought we were on the cusp of something better than I could have dreamed. I mean, we'd opened up about everything, past and present. Then suddenly I was leaving, and I panicked." He picked at a speck on his jeans. "She was right about one thing, though."

"What's that?"

"My life is here. Hers is at the ranch."

Leaning back in his leather office chair, hands clasped atop his trim belly, Reid watched him. "Not long ago, you told me about a conversation you had with your sister where she said she wished she'd had a do-over. Tyler, have you ever considered that perhaps God is giving you a do-over with Audrey?"

Tyler released a frustrated sigh. "Reid, have you not been listening?"

"To every word. So, prior to your final conversation, what were things like between you two?"

Tyler recalled all the fun they'd had, whether they were working together or just hanging out. "Pretty great, actually. Once we bared our souls, we connected on a deeper level. Things were different. Better. We even kissed, the night before I left."

Reid's brow shot up. "A real kiss—like something meaningful—or just a peck?"

Tyler felt the corners of his mouth lifting at the memory. "It was meaningful, alright." At least to him.

"And yet you're ready to give up?" Reid shook his head. "Ty, I never would've taken you for the kind of guy to throw in the towel. I guess she wasn't worth fighting for."

Tyler straightened. "Audrey? Of course she's worth fighting for."

"Then why are you here with me?" Reid righted his chair before calmly smoothing a hand over his desktop. "This little, uh, little *episode* of mine has had me thinking I'd like to step down from the company. Running a business takes up a lot of time. Time I could be spending with my family." He finally looked at Tyler. "And I've realized life is too short not to spend it with the people I love."

The sudden shift in conversation had Tyler narrowing his gaze. While he could totally appreciate Reid's stance, Tyler wasn't in a position to run the company solo. Even if Willow wasn't in the picture, he didn't know if he'd be up to it.

Before he could say anything, though, Reid continued. "While you were gone, I was approached about selling the company. At the time, I said no, but the fella gave me his card in case I changed my mind." Cocking his head, he met Tyler's gaze. "I didn't want to say anything while you were gone. But now that you're back, I'm putting the ball in your court. What do you think? Should we sell? Or do you want to take it over? Possibly find another partner?"

The mention of a partner had Tyler's thoughts turning to Dirk and his reluctance to grow his business.

Except Dirk didn't live in the DFW area. No, he'd soon be living at Legacy Ranch. Exactly where Tyler longed to be. With Audrey and her family.

"I can see your wheels turning."

Tyler looked up to find Reid watching him.

"What are you thinking, Ty?"

"That there's someone I need to talk to before I can give you an answer." He scooted to the edge of his seat. "In the meantime, care to help me come up with a plan to get Audrey back?"

Chapter Sixteen

Audrey white-knuckled the steering wheel of her SUV just after noon Saturday, though her anxiety had nothing to do with the traffic on I-35W. Instead, the closer she drew to the home she and Tyler had once shared, the more she found herself regretting her decision not to let him know she was coming.

But then, when he'd set off for Houston back in October, he hadn't told her he was on his way. Until he discovered she wasn't at her father's office and had no way of knowing where to find her.

At least she'd had the forethought to contact an old girlfriend from college to ask if she could stay with her. Though, if things didn't turn out the way she hoped they would, she might just turn around and go back to the ranch.

With the Fort Worth skyline just ahead, she exited near the county hospital and continued west. Taking in her old neighborhood, she was pleased to discover that even more of the colorful Craftsman and wood-framed bungalows dating back to the turn of the twentieth century had either been revived or were in the process.

Her heart rate picked up as she made the turn onto the street where her former home sat—though the sight of countless Christmas decorations made for a pleasant distraction.

Three blocks later, she spotted the two-bedroom Craftsman with a teal shake gable over pale teal siding and white trim—and Tyler's truck was in the drive.

While her nerves were still aflutter, the memories that washed over her were those of happy times. She and Tyler were a team, both at work and at home. A good one, at that. Until she had allowed something beyond her control to destroy it.

Bringing her vehicle to a stop, she shifted into Park before bowing her head. "Lord, I don't know what You have in store for Tyler and me. What a future together might look like or where it will play out. I just pray that we can be together. Amen."

After checking her look in the rearview mirror, she turned off the engine, then made sure there was no traffic before stepping into the comfortably cool air. She started up the walk, her heart racing, though whether it was anticipation or anxiety, she wasn't quite sure.

Taking in her surroundings, she noticed the crepe myrtle they'd planted at one corner of the house had grown considerably. And the existing shade tree on the opposite side had extended its reach beyond the driveway and over the lawn. Meanwhile, the barren Bartlett pear positioned between the house and the street made her smile as she recalled that last Christmas she'd spent here.

With another bolstering breath, she climbed the trio of steps to the painted wood-plank porch. Then, before she could worry herself anymore, she knocked on the solid wood door painted a shade darker than the teal on the gable.

Soon, she heard movement on the other side. Not surprising. The home wasn't that big. Then the deadbolt clicked, and the door opened.

Tyler just stood there, wearing a gray Rangers T-shirt over faded jeans and bare feet, his light brown eyes wide with surprise.

"Audrey? I—" he dragged his fingers through his already messy hair "—I wasn't expecting you."

His nervousness had her grinning. "Of course you weren't. It's called a surprise visit."

Toying with his scruff of a beard, he said, "It certainly is." He glanced behind him then, as though looking for something. Or maybe just checking the condition of the place. "Come on in." He held the door wider, allowing her to pass.

From her first step, her gaze traversed the inside of the home as memories assailed her. Tyler carrying her over the threshold the day they moved in. Their first Christmas. The day she learned they were going to have a baby.

Shutting down that train of thought, she couldn't help noticing all the boxes scattered throughout the place. But before she could say anything, she heard Willow whimpering. That was when she noticed the baby monitor attached to his belt.

"Sounds like naptime is over," he said.

"I hope I didn't wake her."

"Nah, she was due to wake up anyway." He motioned for her to join him. "C'mon."

She followed him across the original wood floors, through the once-familiar spaces until they reached what had been a combo guest room and office. Though it appeared the desk had been replaced with a crib. This would've been where his sister, Carrie, had stayed with Willow, until her untimely passing.

"Here we are," he said as he approached the white crib with a pink dust ruffle and a pink and gray sheet. "Look who's here, Willow." Lifting her into his arms, he turned toward Audrey.

"Hello, sweet girl."

Willow smiled, waving her little arms.

"Whoa, I think she's happy to see you." He handed the child to Audrey.

Grinning down at the precious bundle, she said, "And I'm happy to see you, too."

"Let me go fix her bottle." When he whisked out of the room, Audrey followed, noticing even more storage containers. "What's with all the boxes?"

"We're going to be moving." At the kitchen's original double-bowl drainboard sink, he added water to a bottle. "I'm hoping to put the house on the market after the first of the year."

"That's a good time to do it. People looking for a fresh start in the new year." She eyed the white cabinets, wood countertops and wood plank ceiling. "So did you decide on a home?"

He added the powdered formula. "No, I decided to rent a house for the time being."

Running a finger over Willow's tiny fist, she said, "I thought you wanted to establish a home for you and Willow?"

"I do." Turning toward her, he twisted the top on. "But there are other aspects of our life—our future—that need to be explored before I can make a decision."

"What aspects?"

"Before I answer that, I have a question for you." After shaking the bottle, he handed it to her. "What brings you to Fort Worth?" And as Willow began greedily sucking, he watched Audrey intently. "Why are you here?"

"To see you." She lifted her gaze to his. "To tell you that I love you, too. And I want to be with you always, even if it means staying here in Fort Worth."

His eyes grew wider. He blinked. "You'd give up your life at Legacy Ranch?"

"The ranch will always be there. We can visit." She smiled. "I hear they have some really cool glamping cabins."

The corners of his mouth twitched. "You don't say." Hands on his hips, he turned away. Cleared his throat. "There's just one problem."

She watched Willow watching her, those tiny fingers opening and closing against Audrey's hand.

"Reid and I have decided to sell our business."

Jerking her attention back to Tyler, she waited for him to continue.

"He wants more time with his family, and now that I have Willow, I don't feel comfortable enough to go it on my own."

"What are you going to do?"

Hands slung low on his hips, he took a long breath. "I've decided to partner with another fellow who has a growing construction business." He looked her way. "Though his passion leans toward restorations."

"I see." She nodded. "Like Dirk?"

Gaze still fixed on her, he said, "It is Dirk."

Her stomach began to flutter as he inched closer.

"A wise man recently told me life is too short not to spend it with the people you love." Looking into her eyes, he cupped her elbow with his hand. "I love you, Audrey. I've never stopped loving you, but I failed to let you know just how much. Then I had the audacity to offer you a wedding at the Justice of the Peace." He feigned a facepalm. "What was I thinking?"

Smiling, she said, "You weren't. You were stressed." She lifted a brow. "Though I was rather upset with you when I saw that you'd left your Christmas decorations behind."

He shrugged. "Sorry. My truck was stuffed and I was in a rush."

She waggled her eyebrows. "Good news—I brought them with me."

"You did?"

"I will not let Willow celebrate her first Christmas without a tree and her stocking."

"Well..." With Willow between them, he looked at her. "We won't be here for Christmas. We were kind of hoping to spend Christmas with you."

Her gaze searched his. "Where will you be?"

"Remember that rental house I told you about?"

She nodded.

"It's just outside of Hope Crossing."

Her heart began to race. "Really?"

"I'll take possession next week."

"So you won't be staying in the log cabin?"

"No. I've monopolized that long enough. It's time to open it up to *paying* guests. Also, I'm going to need to remain here through next week, while Reid and I work out the sales agreement. But come Friday, Willow and I will be headed your way with a trailer full of furniture and household goods."

Her mind was already racing as she contemplated their arrival. "In that case, I don't know if you can take possession of your house any earlier, but if they'll allow it, I can pick up the key and make sure everything is ready for you. Things like groceries and cleaning supplies." And a Christmas tree. She grinned.

"That would be great. I'll see what I can do."

Since Willow had depleted her bottle, Audrey set it aside and moved the child to her shoulder. "In the meantime, can I help you do some packing?"

"Sure." Wearing a mischievous smile, he inched closer. "But first—" he touched a finger to her chin, tilting it upward ever so slightly "—I love you, Mrs. Caldwell."

"And I am over the moon for you, Mr. Caldwell."

Smiling, he touched his lips to hers. And she knew beyond a shadow of a doubt that he was the only man for her.

Christmas Eve day was a whirlwind of activity at the ranch house. People running up and down the stairs, from room to room, wrapping presents, baking, making candy...the sights and sounds of Christmas. And from his seat at the kitchen table where he held Willow in his lap, Tyler took in each and every moment of it.

Christmas at Legacy Ranch was one of the things he'd missed most after he and Audrey split. The love that existed here was unlike any other. At least in his opinion.

"Are you getting settled at your new place, Tyler?" Aunt Dee stood at the counter just after noon, stirring yet another batch of cookies, though he couldn't imagine what. She'd already made molasses, spritz, chocolate crinkles and cutout sugar cookies, which Grayson and Bryce were in the process of decorating on either side of him. And all of that was on top of the fudge and peanut butter balls she'd made and tucked in the refrigerator yesterday.

"I am, thanks to your nieces." While he, Dirk and the boys had offloaded items into the small farmhouse with two bedrooms, one bath, an eat-in kitchen and a living room on Saturday, Audrey and Tessa unpacked, washed and put things away. All amidst the glow of the Christmas tree and mantel decorations Audrey had ready and waiting for him and Willow when they arrived Friday evening.

"Speaking of my nieces, where did Meredith, Tessa and Audrey run off to?"

"They're wrapping presents in our room upstairs." Grayson added red sprinkles to the green frosting on his latest cookie creation. "Mom said it was the only room big enough to hold them *and* all the presents."

"None of which are for you, I'm certain," Aunt Dee teased.

"I hope I get the new Hero Squad movie." Grayson set his cookie aside. "Then I can watch it over and over."

"I want a Hero Squad bike helmet to go with my new bike." Six-year-old Bryce's eyes were wide with anticipation.

"What new bike?" Aunt Dee eyed him curiously.

Glancing over his shoulder, he said, "The one I'm gonna get for Christmas." He swiped more frosting onto his cookie. "At least I hope so."

"Bryce, didn't anyone ever tell you not to count your chickens before they hatch?" his great-aunt asked.

The kid wrinkled his nose. "Huh?"

A loud knock at the front door echoed through the center hall.

Since everyone else was busy, Tyler pushed to his feet. "I'll get that."

"Thank ya, Tyler," Aunt Dee hollered behind him.

He was approaching the door when he glanced over his shoulder to find a smiling Audrey descending the stairs, carrying a small stack of wrapped gifts.

"Who's at the door?" she asked.

Reaching for the knob, he said, "I'm about to find out." Then, as she paused at the bottom step, he swung it open to find the gentleman from Christmas Under the Stars. The one who'd sent Aunt Dee into a tizzy. In his arms, he held a red poinsettia plant and what appeared to be a fancy box of chocolates.

"Mr. Walters." Audrey moved beside Tyler. "Merry Christmas."

"Mark, please. And a Merry Christmas to you all, as well." His blue eyes darted between Tyler and Audrey, pausing on Willow. "What a beautiful baby you have."

Before Audrey could correct Mr. Walters, Tyler smiled and said, "Thank you."

His gaze settling on Audrey, the older man said, "Is your aunt available, by any chance?"

Setting the gifts aside, Audrey smiled. "Why, yes, she is. Follow me."

Having witnessed her aunt's uncharacteristic display of disdain for the man at the bonfire, Tyler followed Audrey and Mark, pausing in the doorway in case Aunt Dee had another negative reaction.

"Aunt Dee?" Audrey said, before stepping aside. "You have a guest."

Wearing a red Baking Spirits Bright apron over a black T-shirt that boasted some other Christmassy phrase, her hair pulled back in a short ponytail, the older woman looked up, her blue eyes widening.

Before she could say anything, the gentleman smiled. "Merry Christmas, D'Lynn."

Wiping her hands on her apron, she rounded the end of the counter, tucking invisible hairs behind her ears as though suddenly self-conscious. "Merry Christmas to you."

"Who's that?" Bryce asked, causing the crimson in his great-aunt's cheeks to intensify.

"Uh, this is an old friend of mine." She finally looked the other man in the eye. "Mr. Walters."

"Who are the flowers for?" Grayson asked.

To his credit, Mr. Walters's gaze was riveted to Aunt Dee's the entire time. "They're for this lovely lady right here." He handed the plant to her before holding up the box. Still watching Dee, he said, "And I hope you still like chocolate."

"Sure as the sun rises every mornin'." Smiling, she took hold of the box. "Thank you." Daring a glance at their audience, she said, "Can I interest you in a cup of coffee and some Christmas cookies?"

"I'd like that very much. Thank you."

The semiretired attorney—as Tyler had learned over lunch—ended up staying well into the afternoon and, to Tyler's surprise, there had been no shortage of conversation between him and Aunt Dee.

Dirk soon joined them, and then Kendall arrived later in the afternoon. As the sky grew dark, they all headed off to church for the six o'clock candlelight service, before returning to the ranch house where they enjoyed tamales and countless Christmas treats while watching *It's a Wonderful Life*. Until Willow grew fussy.

When Tyler reluctantly decided to take her home, Audrey offered to follow them in her own vehicle so they could spend a little more time together. And that suited him just fine.

Then, after Willow was properly outfitted in the Christmas sleeper Audrey had gotten her, they settled on his plush gray sofa amidst no other lights but those on the Christmas tree, Audrey beside him as he fed Willow her bottle. And he could hardly wait to give Audrey the surprise he had tucked beneath the pillow next to him.

Resting her head on his shoulder, she said, "This is one of my favorite things to do. Kind of the calm before the storm tomorrow."

"Ah, but it'll be a good storm. Like snow in Texas."

Her soft chuckle went straight to his heart, making him smile.

"So..." Standing, she moved to the Christmas tree and picked up a gift that could only be from her because there were no other gifts under it. "I have something special for you and Willow."

He smiled at the wide-eyed girl in his arms. "You hear that, Willow. Our first present."

Placing the gift on the sofa, Audrey held out her hands. "Shall we trade?"

"Sure." He passed Willow to her before taking hold of the festively wrapped package. "I wonder what it could be." He held it near his ear and gave it a shake.

"Oh, stop being a goof and open it."

"I'm simply savoring my gift."

"Then savor it a little faster, please."

"You're so impatient." Locating the edge of the paper, he slid a finger beneath it and tore the wrapping off to reveal a plain white box. He lifted the lid and folded back the tissue paper to find a black leather-bound book with a picture of him, Audrey and Willow tucked inside a frame on the cover.

Removing it from the box, he opened it to discover page after page of photos, some of Willow alone, others of him and her, and more of the three of them. He blinked, swallowing the sudden lump in his throat. Given that he had very few photos of his family, an album like this meant the world to him. "This is—" He cleared his throat. "I've never received such a thoughtful gift." Wrapping an arm around her shoulders, he pulled her close and kissed her temple. "Thank you, Audrey."

Looking up at him with tears in her eyes, she said, "You're welcome."

After thumbing through more pages, he set the

book aside before retrieving his and Willow's gift for Audrey. "We have something for you, too." He held up the small gift bag with tissue paper sticking out of it.

She set the bottle on the coffee table. "I think Little Miss is out for the count." Then, sitting back, she moved Willow to her lap. "Okay, I'm ready."

When he handed it to her, she wasted no time reaching inside and pulling out the tissue-wrapped gift. She peeled back the layers until she found the round salt dough ornament with an impression of Willow's hand.

"Aww, her little handprint." She pouted. "This is so precious." Then she turned over the tag attached to the ribbon that had been threaded through a hole for hanging and read, "Will you be my mommy?"

Her eyes went wide. And when they darted to Tyler, he was holding up an engagement ring.

"You said you wanted to adopt. But the thing is, Willow and I are kind of a package deal." He smiled. "We love you, Audrey, and really want you to be a part of our lives forever." Holding up his free hand, he added, "Now, I'm not going to rush you into anything like last time. A proper church wedding takes time to plan, but I can use that time to start rectifying my past mistakes. With God's help, I promise to be real with you. To cherish you as we walk through life together, the good and the bad. To let you see my fears and flaws, no matter how ugly they might be, because you are the best thing that's ever happened to me." He glanced at Willow. "Make that to us. Will you marry me...again?"

The smile on her beautiful face grew bigger by the moment. "In a word, yes." Then she grabbed hold of his collar and pulled him closer until their lips met.

He couldn't help chuckling at her exuberance.

Releasing him, she leaned back, a contented smile on her face. "I don't need another thing for Christmas. Everything I've ever dreamed of is right here."

"I feel the same way." He watched the precious baby girl, sound asleep in Audrey's lap. If it wasn't for her, he and Audrey might never have rediscovered one another. New and improved versions of themselves, made possible only by the grace of God. He'd taken their brokenness and created something new and wonderful. Soon, they'd be a family.

And that was the greatest gift Tyler could ever receive.

* * * * *

*If you enjoyed this book in
Mindy Obenhaus's Legacy Ranch miniseries,
be sure to pick up the first book*

An Unexpected Companion

Available now from Love Inspired!

Dear Reader,

I hope you enjoyed this second visit to Legacy Ranch. Tyler and Audrey were, by all counts, one of those couples who seemed to have everything going for them. Successful careers, a lovely home, a great relationship. But like the house that was built on the sand, when the storms came, the house collapsed. And they were left floundering—until they met Jesus, the only One who can truly heal all our hurts.

There are a lot of hurting people in this world. It doesn't matter how much money you have, the color of your skin or where you live, none of us are immune to life's hardships. The good news is that we don't have to face them alone. Jesus is our "very present help in trouble." If you're struggling, no matter what the issue may be, God can help. He might not take away the pain and agony this life brings, but He's promised to walk through it with you, if you will turn to Him.

My prayer this holiday season is that you will experience the true joy of Christmas. Not in the presents or the decorations—though I do love them—but in the priceless gift of Jesus, and the hope of salvation that only comes from Him.

Until next time, Merry Christmas!
Mindy

Get up to 4 Free Books!

We'll send you 2 free books from each series you try PLUS a free Mystery Gift.

FREE Value Over **$25**

Both the **Love Inspired®** and **Love Inspired® Suspense** series feature compelling novels filled with inspirational romance, faith, forgiveness and hope.

YES! Please send me 2 FREE novels from the Love Inspired or Love Inspired Suspense series and my FREE gift (gift is worth about $10 retail). After receiving them, if I don't wish to receive any more books, I can return the shipping statement marked "cancel." If I don't cancel, I will receive 6 brand-new Love Inspired Larger-Print books or Love Inspired Suspense Larger-Print books every month and be billed just $7.19 each in the U.S. or $7.99 each in Canada. That is a savings of 20% off the cover price. It's quite a bargain! Shipping and handling is just 50¢ per book in the U.S. and $1.25 per book in Canada.* I understand that accepting the 2 free books and gift places me under no obligation to buy anything. I can always return a shipment and cancel at any time by calling the number below. The free books and gift are mine to keep no matter what I decide.

Choose one:
☐ **Love Inspired Larger-Print** (122/322 BPA G36Y)
☐ **Love Inspired Suspense Larger-Print** (107/307 BPA G36Y)
☐ **Or Try Both!** (122/322 & 107/307 BPA G36Z)

Name (please print)

Address   Apt. #

City   State/Province   Zip/Postal Code

Email: Please check this box ☐ if you would like to receive newsletters and promotional emails from Harlequin Enterprises ULC and its affiliates. You can unsubscribe anytime.

Mail to the Harlequin Reader Service:
IN U.S.A.: P.O. Box 1341, Buffalo, NY 14240-8531
IN CANADA: P.O. Box 603, Fort Erie, Ontario L2A 5X3

Want to explore our other series or interested in ebooks? Visit www.ReaderService.com or call 1-800-873-8635.

---

*Terms and prices subject to change without notice. Prices do not include sales taxes, which will be charged (if applicable) based on your state or country of residence. Canadian residents will be charged applicable taxes. Offer not valid in Quebec. This offer is limited to one order per household. Books received may not be as shown. Not valid for current subscribers to the Love Inspired or Love Inspired Suspense series. All orders subject to approval. Credit or debit balances in a customer's account(s) may be offset by any other outstanding balance owed by or to the customer. Please allow 4 to 6 weeks for delivery. Offer available while quantities last.

Your Privacy—Your information is being collected by Harlequin Enterprises ULC, operating as Harlequin Reader Service. For a complete summary of the information we collect, how we use this information and to whom it is disclosed, please visit our privacy notice located at https://corporate.harlequin.com/privacy-notice. Notice to California Residents – Under California law, you have specific rights to control and access your data. For more information on these rights and how to exercise them, visit https://corporate.harlequin.com/california-privacy. For additional information for residents of other U.S. states that provide their residents with certain rights with respect to personal data, visit https://corporate.harlequin.com/other-state-residents-privacy-rights/.

LIRLIS25